By I

You're i

**From turn
palaces—thes
tradition, but romance always rules!**

**So don't miss your VIP invite to the most
extravagant weddings of the year!**

Your royal carriage awaits...

If you love reading stories with a touch of
royalty, don't miss our forthcoming titles in
this miniseries:

CROWNED: AN ORDINARY GIRL
by Natasha Oakley
February 2007

And the next story by Rebecca Winters,
out in April 2007

MATRIMONY WITH HIS MAJESTY

"Sorry I'm late." He spoke into her ear.

Ally jerked her head around, assailed by the familiar scent clinging to his skin.

"Gino—"

She'd never been so happy to see anyone in her life.

"I've missed you too, *bellissima*," he whispered against her lips, before capturing her mouth.

He drew her close, like a lover who'd been anticipating this moment and could no longer hold back.

Ally had been so caught off guard her mouth opened to the urgent pressure of his, and she found herself kissing him back in a slow, languorous giving and taking she'd never experienced in her life.

The background laughter of the crowd faded. All Ally was aware of was the throbbing of her heart against his solid male chest.

THE BRIDE OF MONTEFALCO

BY
REBECCA WINTERS

MILLS & BOON®

All the characters in this book have no existence outside the imagination of the author, and have no relation whatsoever to anyone bearing the same name or names. They are not even distantly inspired by any individual known or unknown to the author, and all the incidents are pure invention.

First published in Great Britain 2006
Harlequin Mills & Boon Limited,
Eton House, 18-24 Paradise Road, Richmond, Surrey TW9 1SR

© Rebecca Winters 2006

ISBN-13: 978 0 263 84938 7
ISBN-10:   0 263 84938 4

Set in Times Roman 12¼ on 14 pt
02-1206-50405

Printed and bound in Spain
by Litografia Rosés, S.A., Barcelona

Rebecca Winters, whose family of four children has now swelled to include three beautiful grandchildren, lives in Salt Lake City, Utah, in the land of the Rocky Mountains. With canyons and high Alpine meadows full of wildflowers, she never runs out of places to explore. They, plus her favourite vacation spots in Europe, often end up as backgrounds for her Mills & Boon® Romance novels, because writing is her passion, along with her family and church. Rebecca loves to hear from her readers. If you wish to e-mail her, please visit her website at: www.rebeccawinters-author.com

Recent titles by the same author:

HAVING THE FRENCHMAN'S BABY*
MEANT-TO-BE MARRIAGE
FATHER BY CHOICE
THEIR NEW-FOUND FAMILY

The Brides of Bella Lucia

CHAPTER ONE

"LIEUTENANT DAVIS?"

The Portland police detective looked up from his computer.

"I'm glad you got here so fast, Mrs. Parker."

"Your message indicated it was urgent."

"It is," he said in a solemn tone. "Come in and sit down."

Ally took a chair opposite his desk.

"I take it there's been a new development in the case."

"Major." He nodded. "The woman who died in the car accident with your husband four months ago has finally been identified through dental records and a DNA match-up."

Though Ally had buried her husband two months ago, she'd needed this day to come if she were ever to find closure. Yet at the same time she'd been dreading it because it meant getting painful facts instead of wallowing in useless conjecture.

"Who was she?"

"A thirty-four-year-old married female from Italy named Donata Di Montefalco."

Finally the woman had a name and a background.

"The Italian authorities have informed me she was the wife of the Duc Di Montefalco, a very wealthy, prominent aristocrat from a town of the same name near Rome. According to the police investigating the case, her husband has had his own people searching for her all these months."

"Naturally," Ally whispered. Had he been in love with his wife? Or had his marriage been unraveling like Ally's?

Though the detective had never said the words, she knew he suspected her husband of having been unfaithful. So had Ally who'd known her marriage was breaking down but hadn't wanted to believe it.

Jim had changed so much from the seemingly devoted family man she'd first married, she'd slowly fallen out of love with him though she wasn't able to pinpoint the exact moment it happened.

During the latter part of their two and half year marriage she'd seen signs that something was wrong. The long absenses from home because of his work, the lack of passion in his lovemaking when he did come home, his disinterest in her life when he made brief, unsatisfactory phone calls home, his desire to put off starting a family until he was making more money.

Despite the fact that there was still no definitive proof of an affair, this news gave added credence to her suspicions.

A fresh stab of pain assailed her. She needed to get out of his office to grieve in private.

Though she'd already had two months to absorb the fact that he hadn't died alone, a part of her had hoped the other woman would have been middle-aged. Possibly an older woman he'd given a lift to because of the storm. But this latest information put that myth to rest. It increased her turmoil that she hadn't loved him as much as she should have, otherwise why hadn't she confronted him before it was too late?

"Thank you for calling me in, Lieutenant." Any second now and she was going to lose control. Living in denial was the worst thing she could have done. Her guilt worsened to recognize she hadn't fought harder to recapture the love that had brought them together in the first place.

"I appreciate what you've done to help me."

She got up to leave. He walked her to the door of his office.

"I'm sorry I had to call you in and remind you of your loss all over again. But I promised to let you know when I had any more information.

"Here's hoping that in the months to come, you'll be able to put this behind you and move on."

Move on? a voice inside her cried hysterically. How did you do that when your husband had died at the lowest ebb in your marriage?

How did you function when your dreams for a happy life with him were permanently shattered?

The detective eyed her with compassion. "Would you like me to walk you out to your car?"

"No thank you," she murmured. "I'll be all right."

She hurried out of his office and down the hall to the front door of the police station.

Dear God—how was it possible things had ended like this? *Nothing* was resolved. If anything, she was riddled with new questions.

Her thoughts darted to the woman's husband. He would have only just learned his wife's body had been found and identified. Besides months of suffering since her disappearance and now this loss, he had to be wondering about Jim's importance in Donata's life.

Wherever the Duc Di Montefalco was at this moment, Ally knew he was in hell.

She could relate…

"Uncle Gino? How come we're going to stay at your farm for a while?"

Rudolfo Giannino Fioretto Di Montefalco, known only to his family and a few close friends as Gino, eyed his eleven-year-old niece through the rearview mirror. The girl sat next to Marcello, Gino's elder brother.

"Because it's summer. I thought you and your father would enjoy getting out in nature instead of being cooped up in the palazzo."

"But what if Mama comes back and we're not there?"

Gino braced himself. The dreaded moment had come.

He pulled up to the side of the farmhouse. In the dying rays of the sun, the cypress trees formed spokes across the yellowed exterior.

He turned in his seat to make certain Sofia was holding her father's hand. Since Marcello had been stricken with Alzheimer's and could no longer talk, it was one of the ways she could express her love and hope to feel his in return.

"I have something to tell you, sweetheart."

A full minute passed. In that amount of time the color had drained from his niece's face. "What is it?" she asked in a tremulous voice. The strain of going months without knowing anything about her mother had robbed Sofia of any joie de vivre.

"Sofia, I have some bad news. Your mama, she was in a car accident, and…she died."

Four months ago in fact, but Gino had only been informed of her death last night. Today he'd been making preparations for Sofia's move to the country with Marcello.

The details surrounding the tragedy were something neither she nor the trusted staff both at the palazzo and the farmhouse needed to know about.

His gaze took in Sofia's pain-filled expression. When his news computed, he heard the sobs of an already heartbroken girl who buried her dark brown head against her father's shoulder.

Marcello looked down at her, not comprehending, not able to comfort his daughter.

Gino felt her sobs from the front seat. Tears welled in his throat. Now that Donata's body had been found and identified, the nightmare of her disappearance was over. But another one had just begun…

His motherless, already introverted niece was going to need more love and understanding than ever.

As for Gino, once he'd arranged with the priest for a private memorial service away from prying eyes so Sofia could say goodbye to her mother in private, he needed to increase security to protect his family from the press.

Carlo Santi, the region's top police inspector and one of their family's best friends was doing his best to stop information from the police department leaking to the various newspapers and media in Rome and elsewhere. But there were those rabid, insatiable vultures from the tabloids who invaded without mercy, always lurking to find something juicy on Gino and his family. It was the price they paid for their title and wealth.

If it weren't for Carlo running interference for him all these months, the situation could have gotten uglier much sooner.

With the sudden debilitating onset of Marcello's disease two years ago, Donata's selfish streak had created havoc in his brother's marriage, and had damaged their daughter irreparably. In Gino's opinion, Donata had to have been one of the world's most insensitive, neglectful wives and mothers on record.

He'd fought hard to protect his brother and niece from the worst of her flaws.

As a result he'd been forced to guard the family secrets with a certain ruthlessness that Donata enjoyed publicizing to anyone who would listen. Her indiscriminate venting had made its way to the press, casting a pall over all their lives, Gino's in particular. Through innuendo she'd made him out to be the grasping, jealous brother-in-law who wanted her and the title for himself.

The only thing Donata hadn't ever considered was her own death.

Once the media got wind of the accident that took her life, everything Gino had done to keep family matters private was about to become a public scandal. The fact that an American man close to Donata's age had been driving the car when they'd been killed provided the kind of fodder to cause a paparazzi frenzy. This kind of story would sell millions of papers with far reaching consequences for Sofia. His niece could be destroyed by the facts, let alone the malicious rumors surrounding them.

Aside from physically removing the two in the back seat to a protected place away from media invasion, there didn't seem to be a thing in hell he could do about unscrupulous journalists digging up old lies on him in order to sell more newspapers. Since his teens, battling the press had been the story of his life. Now it was about to be the story of Sofia's, but not if he could help it!

The orchestra conductor put down his baton. "Take a ten minute break. Then we'll pick up the Brahms at bar 20."

Thankful for the respite, Ally placed her violin on the seat and filed out of the music hall behind the other members of the string section.

She walked down the corridor where she could be alone and reached in her purse for her cell phone.

She was expecting a call back from her doctor. After the meeting with the detective yesterday, she'd developed a migraine that still hadn't gone away. To her dismay there was no message from the doctor. Maybe he'd tried her house phone and had left one.

Sure enough when she retrieved her messages, she learned his nurse had called in a prescription for the pain. If she could just get some relief…

Right now nothing seemed real. The hurt of her failed marriage and the circumstances surrounding Jim's death had gone too deep.

There was one more message, but she'd wait until she got home because the throbbing at the base of her skull refused to let up.

"Ally?" Carol called to her. "Are you all right?"

"I-it's a migraine giving me grief. Do me a favor and tell the maestro I had to go home, but I'll be here in the morning for rehearsal."

The Portland Philharmonic Orchestra's end of May concert was the day after tomorrow.

"I will. Don't worry about your violin. I'll take it home with me and bring it back tomorrow."

"You're an angel."

After getting a drink from the fountain, Ally found the strength to leave the building and head for her car.

Once she'd stopped at the pharmacy where she'd taken one of her pills on the spot, she drove straight home and went to bed with an ice bag across her forehead.

An hour passed before she started to feel a little

better. But there was no pill to stop the questions that wouldn't leave her alone.

For one thing, she wanted to see the place where Jim had died. Her mother hadn't thought it a good idea because visiting the scene of the accident would be too painful.

But Ally couldn't be in any more pain than she was right now. She needed to look at the bridge where Jim's car had skidded on ice into the river. It had happened during a blizzard outside St. Moritz, Switzerland.

She also felt a compulsion to see Donata's family home, maybe even commiserate with the Duc on the phone after she arrived in Montefalco. He wouldn't be human if he didn't have questions, too. Maybe talking together would help both of them cope a little better with the tragedy.

Filled with a sense of purpose she hadn't felt in months, she reached for her cell to phone the airlines. Using her credit card she booked a flight out of Portland for the next day. She would fly to Switzerland, then Italy.

By midafternoon she felt well enough to drive to the bank for traveler's checks. The decision to do something concrete about her situation was probably more therapeutic than taking pills because she found the energy to get packed and arrange for her neighbor to bring in her mail while she was gone.

Once she'd showered, she took another pill and went to bed. When she awakened the next morning she felt considerably better.

With her car safely parked in the garage, all she had left to do was phone for a taxi. While she waited for it to come, Ally listened to the message that had been on her home phone since yesterday morning.

"Hey, Jim! This is Troy at the Golden Arm Gym. Since new management is taking over, we've been cleaning out the lockers. I found something pretty valuable of yours. I don't have a phone number or address on you, so I've been calling all the J., Jim or James Parkers in the city trying to find you. Call me back either way so I can cross you off the list. If you're that Jim, drop by within twenty-four hours or it'll be gone."

Ally had buried her husband two months ago. Just hearing someone ask to speak to him today of all days sent a chill through her body. This call was like a ghost from the past.

Since Jim had never joined a gym, she phoned the number to let them know.

"Golden Arm Gym."

"Is Troy there?"

"Speaking."

"You're the person who called my house yesterday morning. I'm Mrs. James Parker, but I'm afraid you have the wrong Jim Parker."

"Okay. The Jim I'm looking for works in

Europe a lot, and he doesn't have a wife. Thanks for letting me know."

He clicked off, but Ally's fingers tightened around the receiver. Much as she wanted to dismiss his words, she couldn't. Too often in her marriage she'd ignored little signs because she hadn't wanted to believe anything could be wrong.

But those days were over. She was no longer the naïve idealist he'd married.

Once the taxi arrived, she instructed the driver to stop by the gym. It was on the other side of Portland near the freeway leading to the airport. There was no time to lose.

The driver waited while she hurried inside the gym.

When she entered, there were several people already working out. The trainer at the counter flashed her a look of male interest.

"Hi!"

"Hello. Are you Troy?

"That's right."

"I'm Mrs. Parker, the woman you spoke to this morning."

He squinted at her. "I thought you told me I had the wrong person."

"Something you said forced me to reconsider. Did this Jim tell you what kind of work he did in Europe?"

"Yeah. He sells ski wear. In fact we worked out a deal. I gave him free workouts in exchange for his top of the line ski equipment."

She took a fortifying breath. "Then that was my husband."

He blinked. "What do you mean 'was'?"

"Jim died four months ago."

"You're kidding. So that's why I haven't seen him around. What happened?"

"He died in a car accident."

Had there been other women before Donata, and she'd happened to be the unlucky one who'd gone off the bridge with him?

"I'm sorry, Mrs. Parker. Maybe I misunderstood about him not being married."

She shook her head. "No. I'm quite sure you didn't. When did he join this club?"

"About a year ago."

A whole year?

Struggling to remain composed, she pulled the wallet from her purse. Inside was a little photo holder. She showed him the one of Jim.

The other man stared at it, then nodded. "Just a sec and I'll get what he left here."

Half a minute later he came out of his office with an unfamiliar looking silver laptop. The power cord had been taped to it.

He tore the attached slip in half. "Sign here."

Ally complied, trying her best not to tremble.

"Thank you for the call, Troy. I'm anxious to keep anything that belonged to my husband."

"Of course. I'm glad you came when you did, otherwise we'd have sold it. I really am sorry about your husband."

"So am I," she muttered in a dull voice.

She'd known nothing about the purchase of this laptop. Jim's company had supplied him with the one he'd always used to do business.

The only reason for this computer to exist meant he'd had something to hide.

She would have to take it to Europe with her. She didn't have time to go back home. After she returned to the States, she'd look inside. If she discovered painful secrets, hopefully by then she'd be better able to handle them.

After going out to the cab, she packed the laptop in her suitcase then told the driver to step on it.

As she sat back in the seat, she shuddered to realize that her husband had been working out in a gym for eight months, and she'd had no knowledge of his activities. He must have stopped by either coming or going to Switzerland on business.

It was one thing to recognize that the two of them had drifted apart, but quite another to realize he'd been living a separate and secret life. How humiliating to be confronted by the truth in front of Troy, a total stranger to her.

Oh, Jim. What happened to the man I married? Did I ever really know you?

Ally was beginning to wonder…

With the aid of the staff, Gino helped his grieving Sofia and her father into the limo outside the local parish church. They'd just buried Donata in the adjacent cemetery. It had all been carried out in secret while word of her death had finally been announced by the media.

One day when the furor had died down, he would have her remains removed and buried on the grounds of the Montefalco estate in the family plot.

"I'll join you at the farm in a few minutes, sweetheart."

Sofia's face was ravaged by fresh tears. "Don't take too long."

"I promise. I just want to say goodbye to a few people and thank the priest."

She nodded before the farmhouse caretaker Paolo drove the car away.

Vastly relieved this part was over, he turned swiftly to Carlo whom he'd asked to wait until they could talk in private.

"The onslaught has started in earnest, Carlo."

"What's going on?"

"One of the security guards at the palazzo just left a message that a woman claiming to be Mrs. James Parker tried to get in to see Marcello a few minutes ago. It's another ploy on the part of the paparazzi to ruin my family."

The other man pursed his lips. "I must say I'm surprised they'd be audacious enough to impersonate the wife of the deceased."

Gino grimaced. "Nothing surprises me anymore. She came in a taxi. As a precaution, the guard wrote down the license plate number."

Carlo's brows lifted. "Want me to track her down and have her vetted?"

Gino was way ahead of him.

"If you could locate her, I'd like to do the interrogating for a change."

"What's your plan?"

"How long could she be held at the jail?"

"Only twelve hours. If you can't make the charges stick, then we'd have to release her."

Gino's eyes glittered. "Don't worry about that. She's going to wish she'd never ventured into my territory."

Carlo pulled out his pocket notepad. "Give me the plate number. I'll alert the desk sergeant at the jail to cooperate with you."

"As usual, I'm indebted to you."

"Our families have been close for years. I'm not about to see you and Sofia destroyed."

Those words meant more to Gino than his friend would ever know.

"*Grazie*, Carlo."

* * *

There was a jarring knock on the bedroom door.

"Signora Parker?"

Ally had only been in bed an hour and groaned in disbelief. Her long connecting flights from Oregon to Switzerland, then Rome, had been bad enough. But it was the horrendous day she'd spent on a hot, overcrowded train to reach the hilltop town of Montefalco that had done her in.

To compound her troubles, every hotel in the town had been booked months in advance for some festival. If her taxi driver hadn't taken pity on her and brought her to his sister's house to sleep, she would have been forced to return to Rome for the night. Perish the thought!

The rapping grew louder.

"Signora!"

Ally couldn't work out what was happening.

"Just a moment!"

She sat up, unconsciously running a hand through her short, blond curls. They made her look younger than her twenty-eight years.

Grabbing her robe lying across the end of the bed, she slipped it on, then hurried over to the door and opened it.

The elderly woman looked tired. Ally thought she sounded out of breath.

"Quickly! You must get dressed! A car from the Palazzo Di Montefalco has come for you."

Ally's green eyes widened. "But that's impossible!"

Earlier in the day she'd been turned away from the palace gates by armed guards. No one knew where she'd gone after she'd gotten back in the taxi.

"You have to be a very important person for the Duc Di Montefalco himself to send for you. Hurry! You must not keep the driver waiting,"

"I'll be out as soon as I can. Thank you."

Unless one of the guards had followed the taxi here, Ally was mystified as to how he'd known where to find her.

But that didn't matter now. In a few minutes she was finally going to meet with the man she'd flown thousands of miles to see. After her futile attempts to reach him by phone from Rome before boarding the train, and then the fiasco that took place earlier in front of the palace, she'd almost given up hope.

She shut the door and reached for her suitcase. In a few minutes she'd donned fresh jeans and a green print blouse. At one-thirty in the morning she didn't feel like dressing in the suit she'd brought.

Once she'd put on her sneakers, she finished the little packing she had to do. Before leaving the room, she found her purse and left two hundred dollars on the dresser.

One more look around to make sure she hadn't left anything behind and she joined the older woman who stood in the foyer waiting.

Ally rushed up to her. "I'm so sorry you had to be wakened at this late hour because of me. Especially after you were kind enough to take me in. I've left money on the dresser for you and your brother. Thank you again for everything, including the delicious meal and the chance to shower. Please tell your brother thank you, too. I don't know what I would have done without your help."

The other woman nodded impatiently. "I'll tell him. Now you must go!"

She opened the door onto an ancient narrow alley. The woman's house was one of several built at street level. Yet all Ally could see was a gleaming black sedan parked right outside the door.

The light from the foyer illuminated the gold falcon insignia of the Montefalco crest emblazoned on the hood.

As Ally ventured over the threshold, a man dressed in black like the palace security guards stepped away from the stone wall connecting the houses.

Since Ally was only five foot five, she was immediately aware of a tall, solidly built male with hair black as night. Something about his imposing demeanor and the almost hawkish features that distinguished him from so many other Italian male faces she'd seen today sent a little shiver of alarm through her body.

With breathtaking economy of movement he relieved her of her purse and suitcase.

"Give that back!" she cried. Ally tried to wrest the suitcase from his hand, but it was no use. She was no match for him. Besides, he'd already stashed everything in the trunk.

She felt his glance mock her before he opened the rear door.

The interior light revealed a broad shouldered man of unquestionable strength. The sun had darkened his natural olive toned skin. He was more than conventionally handsome. The words splendid and fierce came to Ally's mind before she climbed in the back seat.

Following that thought she wondered if she wasn't crazy to let a total stranger whisk her away from her only place of refuge in this foreign country. She didn't know a soul here except the taxi driver and his sister.

Worse, she'd somehow lost her cell phone during the train ride, so she couldn't call for help. Someone had probably pilfered it.

The premonition that she might need a phone to the outside world was growing stronger as he climbed in behind the wheel and set the locks.

After he turned on the engine, they shot down the empty alley to the main road. Three blocks later and Ally sensed she was in trouble.

Instead of climbing to the top of the hill, the

driver drove them through the lower streets of the town. He appeared to have a destination in mind that wasn't anywhere near the ochre-colored ducal palace clinging to the side of the cliff.

Rather than leave the old woman's protection at such an unorthodox hour, Ally should have obeyed her instincts and stayed in her room until morning.

She leaned forward in the leather seat. "This isn't the way to the palace." She'd said it in as steady a voice as she could muster.

"Please take me back to that woman's house."

The enigmatic guard ignored her demand and kept driving until they entered another alley behind some municipal buildings.

"Where are you taking me?"

"All in good time, *signora*." The first words out of his mouth were spoken in impeccable English with only a slight trace of accent.

He pulled in front of a steel door with a single light shining overhead. In the next instant he'd come around to her side of the car and opened the door for her.

"After you, *signora*."

She lifted her proud chin, refusing to budge. "Where have you brought me?"

His heavily lashed eyes looked like smoldering black fires.

"The Montefalco police station."

Police? "I don't understand."

"Earlier this evening you asked to speak to the Duc Di Montefalco, did you not?"

"Yes. Are you telling me I didn't have the right?"

"Let's just say he doesn't grant interviews."

"I didn't want an interview. I've flown a long way to talk to him in private."

He shifted his weight, drawing her attention to the play of raw muscle power in his arms and chest.

"Anyone who wants to make contact with him has to go through me."

That explained why she could never get anywhere on the phone or in front of the security guards.

Ally couldn't prevent her gaze from traveling over his distinctive masculine features. Those piercing eyes were framed by startlingly black brows. Never had she looked into such an arresting face.

"Are you a police officer who doubles as one of his bodyguards or something?"

A dangerous smile curled the corners of his mocking mouth. "That's one way of describing me."

CHAPTER TWO

A STRANGE chill rippled across Ally's skin. "How did you know where to find me?"

"The guards took down the license plate of your taxi. A simple phone call to the driver told me what I needed to know."

As easy as that.

"I told the palace guards who I was. They didn't even try to help me."

His lips twisted unpleasantly. "Any woman could claim to be Mrs. James Parker."

"But that's who I am! I have my passport to prove it."

"Passports are a dime a dozen. I believe that's the American expression."

She shook her head in exasperation. "Why are you being so hateful to me? I came to Italy expressly to meet with Mr. Montefalco for very personal reasons. You act like I've committed some crime."

"Trespassing *is* a crime," he muttered just loud enough to heighten her anxiety.

"This is impossible! I demand you call the American Embassy and let me talk to someone in charge."

His mouth formed a contemptuous line.

"No one there will be available before morning."

"In America you're innocent until proven guilty!" she flung at him, starting to feel desperate.

"Then you should have stayed there, or wherever you really came from, *signora*," he retorted in a voice of ice.

Trapped and painfully tired, Ally made the decision not to fight him. He was too formidable an adversary. This was all a terrible mistake, the kind you were supposed to be able to laugh about after you'd returned home from being abroad.

Once this man went through her belongings and found out the truth of her identity, she didn't expect an apology. However she could hope for a quick release and the chance to talk to Mr. Montefalco before too much more time passed.

Wrapping her dignity around her like a cloak, she got out of the car and waited for him to open the door.

He pressed a button on the wall of the building. In a minute the door swung open electronically.

She'd never been inside a jail of any kind. In

the small reception area there were two armed police officers, one of them seated at a desk.

They nodded to her captor.

After an exchange in Italian she couldn't possibly understand, he left her in their charge and disappeared out the door.

"Wait—" she called out to no avail.

At that point she was photographed, finger-printed and escorted down a passageway to a tiny room with a cot and a chair.

The door closed behind her, leaving her to her own devices.

The whole situation was so surreal, she wondered if she was hallucinating on the painkiller she'd taken before going to bed. It had been a pre-ventive measure to ward off another sick headache.

Suddenly she heard the click of the electronic lock and the door opened. She swung around in time to see the driver who'd abducted her step inside. The door shut behind him, enclosing her in this tiny closet of a holding cell with a man who could overpower her before she took her next breath. He'd brought her purse with him.

"During your interrogation you have your choice of the chair or the bed, *signora*."

She was feeling pretty hysterical about now.

"I'd rather stand."

"So be it."

He opened her purse. After examining the

contents including her wallet and bottle of medication, he pulled out her passport.

She watched him study the picture that had been taken three years earlier. At that point in time she'd been a radiant fiancée with long blond hair and sparkling green eyes, anticipating a skiing honeymoon in the French Alps with Jim.

Ally could no longer relate to that person.

The stranger's enigmatic gaze flicked to her face and hair. He scrutinized her as if trying and failing to find the woman in the photo.

He put the passport in his pocket, then tossed her purse with its contents on the cot next to the pathetic looking lump that was supposed to be a pillow.

Only now did she realize her suitcase was still in his car.

"I'd like my luggage. There are things I need," she explained. "I have to have it, you know? Like clean clothes?"

"First things first, *signora*. Until I get the answers I'm looking for, we'll be at this all night. Since you already appear unsteady on your feet— no doubt from fear that you've been caught in the act—I suggest you sit down before you pass out."

"In the act of what?" Ally questioned, totally shocked by his assumption she'd done something wrong.

"We both know you're one of the unscrupulous

paparazzi, willing to do anything for an exclusive. But I'm warning you now. After trying to impersonate someone else, you're facing a prison sentence unless you start talking."

"I *am* Mrs. James Parker."

"Just tell me the name of the tabloid that sent you on this story."

Heat swept through her body into her face. "You're crazy!" she blurted in exasperation. "My name is Allyson Cummings Parker. I'm an American citizen from Portland, Oregon. I only arrived in Rome from Switzerland this afternoon, or—or yesterday afternoon. I'm all mixed up now about the time. But I'm the widow of James Parker. He was a ski clothes salesman who worked for an American manufacturing company called Slippery Slopes of Portland. He died in a car accident outside St. Moritz, Switzerland, with Mr. Montefalco's wife four months ago!"

"Of course you are," he said in a sarcastic aside that made her hackles rise.

Her breathing grew shallow.

"Since you tracked me down through the taxi driver, he'll tell you he picked me up at the train station, and had to do all the translating while I tried to find a room because I don't speak Italian."

Her captor nodded. "He admitted you put on a convincing performance. That is…until you gave yourself away by asking him to drive you to the palazzo. That was your fatal mistake."

Her hands curled into fists. "How else was I supposed to talk to Mr. Montefalco? He doesn't list his phone number. When I reached Rome, I was on the phone with an Italian operator for half an hour trying to get a number for him."

"He doesn't talk to strangers. If you were an innocent tourist who didn't have a place to spend the night, you would have been much more concerned about that than brazenly attempting to ramrod your way into the ducal palace that has always been off limits to the public."

"But I didn't know that!"

"You're a good liar, I'll grant you that, but it was a dangerous act of idiocy on your part no matter how greedy you are for money. It's the one credential you sleazy members of the media carry every time you trespass on sacred ground for a story. You have no decency or thought for the precariousness of the situation. None of your kind has a conscience."

He folded his arms, eyeing her with chilling menace.

"As you're going to find out, I don't have one, either. So you can start talking now, or look forward to being incarcerated here indefinitely."

Her mouth had gone dry. "You're going to be sorry you're treating me like this," she warned him with a mutinous expression. "When Mr. Montefalco finds out I'm here anxious to talk to him, you'll be lucky if it's only your job you lose."

His black eyes felt like lasers, scanning beneath the surface for any abnormalities.

"Who sent you to do their dirty work?" he rapped out as if she hadn't spoken. "Tell me now and I'll use my influence with the judge to get you off with a light sentence."

A pulse throbbed at the corner of his hard jaw. He was in deadly earnest. That made the situation so much worse for Ally.

She spread her hands. "Look—there's been a huge misunderstanding here. If you think my passport and driver's license are doctored, then look at my airline tickets again. It proves I just flew here from Portland, with a stopover in Switzerland to see where my husband's accident happened."

His gaze searched hers relentlessly. "You call that proof when you could have flown from Italy to Oregon on your tabloid's money to begin your impersonation? You're wasting my time."

He pressed a button above the door, no doubt sending a signal that he was ready to leave. This was a nightmare!

"No—don't go yet—" she begged as the door swung outward.

He paused in the aperture, almost filling it with his tall, powerful body.

"Please—" she beseeched him. "There's someone you could call who will vouch for me. His name is L—"

She broke off talking because she suddenly realized she didn't want him to talk to Lieutenant Davis. She would be too embarrassed for the detective to know she'd flown here to satisfy her curiosity about Donata. It was a private matter she'd rather no one else knew about. Until she talked to Mr. Montefalco, it was absolutely crucial her activities and whereabouts remain a secret to everyone including her mother. Ally's mom thought she was spending the weekend with friends from the orchestra. If she knew the truth, there would have been a battle Ally couldn't have handled.

"Yes?" her adversary mocked again. "You were saying?"

He stood still as a tree trunk. By now she was so beside herself she felt light-headed. Her ears started to buzz.

Out of self-preservation she sank down on the end of the cot and lowered her head so she wouldn't faint.

"Anything you'd like to confess before lights out, *signora*?" he asked without an ounce of concern or compassion.

His voice sounded far away. Ally had to wait

until the worst of her weakness had passed before she could talk.

By then, he'd gone…

Vaguely disturbed by the woman's insistence that she really was the wife of Donata's last lover, Gino sped faster than was prudent through the dark streets toward his family home at the top of the mount. He wanted total privacy before searching the woman's suitcase. En route he phoned Carlo.

"Thank you for helping me carry out my plan. The suspect is in her cell, but I realize we won't be able to hold her for long. I asked the desk sergeant to run her passport through the scanner for verification, then report to you. Do me a favor and let me know what he finds out. When we've learned it's counterfeit, I'll expose her in my own way so she never gets another job. I'm sick of the media."

Once they'd hung up, he used his remote to enter the estate.

After slipping in a private side entrance to the palazzo with his prisoner's luggage, he entered Marcello's study and set it on one of the damask couches.

Upon opening it, he was surprised to see how lightly she traveled. The interior was redolent of her flowery scent. There were only a few changes of outfits and feminine underclothing, all modest and for the most part American brands.

Frowning because he couldn't find a camera or film, in fact nothing that sent up a red flag, his hands dug deeper.

"What's this?"

He felt something solid, wrapped in a towel.

"I knew it!" he whispered fiercely as he pulled out a silver laptop.

No wonder she'd wanted to hold on to her luggage.

He carried it over to the desk and plugged it into the wall adaptor.

"You and your paper are about to be exposed. Believe me, *signora*, you're going to pay—"

He turned it on, then sat down in the leather chair and waited to see what flashed on the screen.

He was ready to seize on anything that linked her to one of the tabloids.

Her home page popped up. He immediately clicked on her favorite pictures icon. Before long he came face-to-face with photos of Donata.

Gino let out a curse. He counted thirty pictures showing his sister-in-law in various stages of dress and undress. The outdoor pictures had been taken in Prague. He recognized the landmarks.

How in the hell had that impossibly green-eyed imposter gotten hold of these?

Donata, Donata.

He gritted his teeth. If these were to make it

onto the streets... If Sofia were ever to see them...

He felt his gut twist in reaction.

There was only one reason why the champagne-blonde with the voluptuous curves locked up in the cell hadn't gone public with them yet. Perhaps she'd decided to approach Marcello first to extort more money from him than her paper would pay out.

Sick to the depth of his being because he knew these photos were only the tip of the iceberg, he packed up the laptop, closed her suitcase and carried both out to the truck he kept on the estate.

Leaving by a hidden road that came out on a side street, he headed for the jail.

Later at the farmhouse when he had the luxury of time, he'd delve into the e-mails and other secrets of the computer's hard drive. Until then, Gino would break her down until she was grist.

He wanted the name of the tabloid she worked for, how many more photos existed and the length of time she'd been on Donata's trail in order to obtain those particular photos.

Ally heard the door open. When she saw a tall dark figure coming toward her before it closed again, she let out a bloodcurdling scream and pulled the sheet over her head. "Nightmares, *signora*?" sounded the devilish voice of her captor. "With the kinds of things you have on your conscience, I can't say I'm surprised."

"Get out!" she shouted into the darkness. "The only person I'll speak to is a diplomat from the American Embassy. Do you understand me?"

"I'm afraid you're going to have a long wait."

She heard something scrape against the cement floor. She shivered to realize he'd pulled the chair next to her bed and had sat down.

"What you're doing is against the law!"

He gave a caustic laugh.

Fear of a sort she'd never known before emboldened her to say the first thing that came into her mind.

"What a tragedy that such a lovely, beautiful town produces monsters like you."

The rhythm of his breathing changed, letting her know she'd struck a nerve. Good!

"For someone in your kind of trouble," he began in a frighteningly silky voice, "I'd advise you to stop fantasizing and tell me everything before the chief prosecutor of the region gets here and you're arraigned before the magistrate."

She sat up on the cot and pressed herself into the corner of the wall, as far away from him as possible.

"Whether you believe me or not, I'm Mrs. James Parker. So far, all you've told me is that I trespassed. But I don't see how I did that when the guards wouldn't let me past the gate."

She heard him shift in the chair.

"If you're telling the truth, and you really are the hapless wife who was the last person to know what your husband was up to, explain what those pictures are doing in your laptop."

Pictures? Ally rubbed her bloodshot eyes with her palms. She was so desperately tired, maybe she was dreaming this horror story.

"I asked you a question, *signora*."

No—she wasn't dreaming. He was sitting there next to her, intimidating her by his very presence. All two hundred pounds of him, hard as steel physically and every other way.

"It's my husband's laptop. I don't know anything about any pictures."

She heard a sharp intake of breath.

"So you carried his laptop with you all the way to Montefalco for no particular reason?"

"I didn't say that!" she protested. "I told you earlier that I came to have a private talk with Mr. Montefalco and no one else."

"In order to show him the photographs and extort thousands of dollars in the process."

Thousands of dollars? What pictures would be worth that kind of money? She took a deep breath, scared of what she might discover.

"If there are pictures, I haven't seen them."

At her hotel in St. Mortiz, Ally would have looked inside the laptop, but she hadn't brought an adaptor to fit in the foreign outlet and figured she would have to wait until she returned to Portland. Part of her knew that was just an excuse. She didn't want to know.

"I planned to talk to him about things that aren't your business or anyone else's."

After a pause, he said, "You can tell me. I have his ear."

"Prove it! For all I know you're just a lowly policeman pretending to be Mr. Montefalco's bodyguard."

Suddenly he was on his feet. She could feel his rage as he pushed the chair away. She hid her face behind the sheet even though it was dark in the room.

Still bristling she said, "Now *you* know how it feels to be told you're a liar and a sleazy con artist out to cash in on someone's private tragedy. I repeat." Her voice throbbed. "I'm *not* saying another word until I can speak to someone from the Embassy."

While she waited for his response, the door opened, then slammed shut.

The next thing she knew the light in her cell went on.

She checked her watch, which she'd changed to Italian time on the train. It said 7:30 a.m.

How long were they going to leave her in here before allowing her to freshen up?

In desperation she dragged the chair over to the door so she could push the button he'd pressed earlier.

Suddenly the door swung open, almost causing her to fall.

A guard she didn't recognize waited for her to climb down, then ordered her to follow him.

She grabbed her purse and trailed him down the hall and around the corner to the bathroom. There was no sign of her captor. She sincerely hoped she would never have to see or talk to him again.

After brushing her hair and putting on some lipstick, she felt a little more human. When she emerged minutes later, the guard escorted her back to her cell where a tray of food was waiting on the chair.

Just looking at the chair reminded her how her interrogator had shoved it across the room in a fit of anger.

In spite of the precariousness of her situation, the fact that she'd been able to infuriate him caused her to smile.

The guard noted it before disappearing.

Locked in once more, her gaze fell on the sparse continental breakfast. Rolls and coffee. But she wasn't about to complain. It might be a long time before she was allowed to eat again, so she consumed everything in short order.

She kept thinking about those pictures he'd

mentioned. Jim had evidently stored some in one of his files. Maybe they were photos of all the women he'd had affairs with in Europe. At this juncture she didn't put anything past him. Her husband had truly lived a double life.

Ally let out a sound of abnegation.

What a fool she'd been not to have confronted him when she'd first suspected there was another woman.

Her abductor's words stung more than ever.

If you're telling the truth, and you really are the hapless wife who was the last person to know what your husband was up to, explain what those pictures are doing in your laptop.

Ally hadn't been hapless. It was a case of not wanting to admit something was wrong and have her mother say, "I told you so. A man with good looks and knows it can't be satisfied with one woman."

Ally didn't believe that. She knew too many attractive couples who had wonderful marriages.

Hers had started out that way, but when she saw changes happening, she should have questioned him point-blank. But she'd been scared. They could have talked things out and maybe salvaged their marriage. Now it was too late. There was no use wishing she'd acted on her suspicions a long time ago.

She looked around her claustrophobic cell. What she needed to do was get out of here.

Her abductor was waiting for her to cooperate. Maybe if she made up a lie, he'd believe her and allow her to go free with a slap on the wrist.

Without hesitation she pushed the chair over to the door and climbed up to press the button.

While she waited for a response, she put it back against the wall.

In a minute the door swung open to reveal the guard who'd brought her breakfast.

"*Signora?*"

"I hate it in here and I'm ready to talk."

He took the tray off her bed and started out the door.

"Did you hear me?" she cried. "I'm ready to confess!"

He shot her an oblique glance before the door closed.

"Ooh—" She pounded her fists against it. "What kind of a lunatic place is this?" she shouted.

When she realized she was only hurting herself, she gave it up and walked around her cell, trying to rub the pain from the sides of her hands.

Five minutes later she experienced déjà vu to hear the door open and see her captor enter the room. When she glimpsed the forbidding look in those fiery black eyes, she backed away from him.

"You're ready to tell the truth, *signora?*"

"Yes, but not in here. I can't abide enclosed places."

He gave an elegant shrug, reminding her what an amazing physique he had.

"It's either in here, or not at all."

"Oh all right!" She took a deep breath. "It's true I pretended to be Mrs. Parker to get the duc's attention.

"I do freelance stories for a local magazine in Portland. One of my boyfriends works for the police department and once in a while he tells me something interesting.

"A couple of months ago he told me his boss was working on a missing persons case involving a married man from Portland and another woman who died with him in Europe. Just the other day he mentioned that they'd finally identified the woman and had pictures of her.

"I asked him if he would let me see them. He did, so I scanned them and downloaded them to my laptop.

"All I wanted to do was talk to the woman's husband and ask if I could do an exclusive story on him. In case he didn't believe I was serious, I planned to show him the pictures. But I wouldn't have allowed them to be published, or have bribed him for money. I just wanted to write about his heart-wrenching ordeal. Americans love stories about wealthy, titled people with problems. It makes them feel better about their own less glorious lives.

"So now that you know the truth, please let me go. All I want is my passport and suitcase back. If you'll send for a taxi, the driver will take me to the train.

How about it? You let me out of here and I'll go straight home to Portland."

His eyes held a frightening gleam.

"You're lying through your pearly-white teeth, *signora*, but I give you credit for your amazing resourcefulness."

His wintry smile daunted her. "As it happens, I never told you the nature of those photos. If you'd known what they contained, you wouldn't have placed your source's job in jeopardy. All you've done is convince me you're a liar."

He was bluffing…

"How typical," she mocked. "If I were a man, you would have said 'good try.' But since I'm a woman, I can't be trusted."

One black brow quirked.

"Aren't you? So far you've told me two diametrically opposing lies, none of which hold water. While I'm still here, want to try for a third? I have nothing more important to do for the moment."

"Okay." She felt all the stuffing go out of her. "I'll

make a deal with you. I'll give you a hundred dollars if you'll let me go. No one will need to know."

"If it were a hundred thousand dollars, I wouldn't take it."

He was impossible!

"Look— All I wanted to do was speak to Mr. Montefalco. This is between him and me, no one else."

He pursed his lips. "Why is that, *signora*?"

She lifted solemn eyes to his.

"Because it's very sad and very personal."

He put his hands on hips, the picture of the ultimate male. "I'm his closest confidant. You can tell me anything. If it will make you feel any better, you can whisper it to me. I promise it will remain sacrosanct."

Something in his tone had her halfway believing him, but it didn't matter.

"How do I know you're not wearing a listening device?"

"You don't," he clipped out. "You'll have to trust me."

She leaned close to him. "Sorry, but I have to talk to him alone."

The nearness of her heart-shaped mouth and the flowery scent her body gave off, stunned him as much as the words that fell from those enticing lips underlining her intransigence.

She couldn't be Mrs. James Parker. Any man married to her wouldn't have felt the urge to turn to Donata or any other woman for that matter.

"If you won't let me out of here," she continued in a low voice, "then bring Mr. Montefalco to me. I want to talk to him, and I believe he'll be anxious to talk to me. We might find we're a comfort to each other."

With his body still reacting to the warmth of her breath on his ear, Gino found himself reluctant to put distance between them. But he had to no matter how much the imploring look in her eyes and the haunting appeal in her voice persuaded him to believe she was finally telling him the truth.

He'd just stepped away, rubbing the back of his neck in an unconscious gesture of frustration when the door opened to reveal one of the guards. He informed Gino that Inspector Santi wanted him on the phone.

Without saying a word to her, he strode down the hall to the office, hardening himself against her sound of protest. In truth he was oddly reticent to find out she was the beautiful dust of the enemy.

He picked up the receiver, then turned his back toward the desk sergeant.

Knowing the jail phone was tapped he said, "Inspector? I'll call you back on my phone." After replacing the receiver, Gino pulled out his cell and rang him on the other man's private line.

Keeping his voice low he said, "Carlo? What did you find out?"

"She *is* Mrs. Parker, Gino."

While his thoughts took off in a dozen directions, Carlo kept talking. "I guess I'm not surprised. She's a widow grieving for her husband."

Gino had proof of that. He'd just come from her cell. She'd claimed that she'd sought out Marcello in the hope of giving and receiving comfort. But if that was true, how did she explain the laptop? Something didn't ring true.

"She said she'd been in St. Moritz to visit the scene of the accident," Gino murmured.

"It's unfortunate she chose this time to come to Italy when the press is just waiting for anything they can do to sensationalize this case. She's the last person *you* should be seen with."

Gino agreed. All it would take was a photo of the two of them together caught by one of the lurking paparazzi, and the hellish situation would escalate overnight.

"You need to leave the jail and let me handle this, Gino. I'll instruct the sergeant to free her. One of the guards will escort her to Rome by train and put her on the next plane for the States."

Gino grunted a response as he listened to his friend. Though Carlo made a lot of sense, Gino couldn't forget that Mrs. Parker had come all this way with that laptop to see Marcello for a specific reason. Since she'd put herself in jeopardy to accomplish her objective, Gino couldn't let her go until he'd found out what was so important she'd risked everything, even jail, to make contact.

"I'm sure you're right, Carlo. I'll leave it up to you."

"That's good. You need to stay as far removed from her as possible."

He would as soon as he'd had time to talk to her away from other people. "*Grazie*, Carlo. It seems that's all I ever say to you."

"Forget it. *Ciao*, Gino."

Ally had been sitting on the cot wondering what was going on when the door flew open.

It was the same guard as before.

"Come, *signora*. You've been released. Please to follow me."

Hardly able to believe it, she grabbed her purse and started after him.

"What about my suitcase?"

"It is here," he said once they'd reached the reception area of the jail.

Convinced her abductor had confiscated the laptop, she leaned over to open the catches and sure enough, she discovered it was gone.

For some inexplicable reason, which was absurd considering her circumstances, she wished he were still here so that in front of his colleagues, she could accuse him of absconding with it.

She shut the lid and lifted her head. "What about my passport?"

"You'll be given it after you board your flight for the U.S."

She almost blurted that she couldn't leave Montefalco yet, but she stopped herself in time. All she needed was to make that mistake and then be shuffled back to her cell for defying him.

She took a deep breath to calm down. When she boarded her jet, she would claim to be ill and ask to be put on a later flight. Once she found a hotel room in Rome, she would figure out another plan to reach Mr. Montefalco.

"Very well. I'm ready whenever you are."

The jail door swung open. Another guard stood outside in front of a white police car and held the rear door open for her. Unlike her captor, he didn't help her with her luggage. No doubt he considered her a lowlife reporter who didn't deserve common courtesy.

She pushed her case across the seat and climbed in.

When their car emerged from the alley, throngs of tourists filled the walkways. The guard wound his way through the charming streets for the short ride to the depot.

She hated the thought of another hot train ride, but there was no help for it.

"Come, *signora*."

The guard had parked the car in a VIP zone. He escorted her through the crowded station and out to the quay.

After a brief talk with one of the conductors, he boarded the train with her and put her in a second class compartment already filled except for one seat in the middle. She had to put her suitcase on the shelf above without his assistance.

"I'll be in the corridor until we reach Rome, *signora*." The warning that she shouldn't try anything to escape was implicit.

Her cheeks hot with anger, she sat down, trying to avoid the interested stares of the other passengers.

No sooner had the guard stepped out of the compartment and disappeared than the train began to inch forward.

Ally was so exhausted after spending a wretched night in that jail cell, she rested her head against the back of the seat. Dispirited by everything that had happened, she closed her eyes for a few minutes, needing sleep. The first thing she would do when she could finally be alone in a hotel room was to crash.

Soon she lost track of time and was almost out for the count when she felt a hand on her arm.

"Signora?" sounded a deep male voice with a vaguely familiar timbre.

She came awake with a cry of alarm.

When she saw her striking captor still dressed in black, standing there bigger than life carrying her suitcase, the breath rushed from her lungs. She blinked up at him, wondering if he was real, or if she was dreaming.

"W-what's going on?"

His hooded eyes played over her features, awakening her senses in spite of her fatigue, or maybe because of it.

"I relieved the other guard. We're getting off at the next stop. Come with me."

Though she felt so groggy she didn't know how she'd be able to walk, she realized this man was her only chance to get Jim's laptop back, and maybe find an entrée to Mr. Montefalco.

Clutching her purse, she got up and followed him out of the compartment and down the corridor. The train had already begun to slow down.

When it came to a stop, several people were waiting to climb on board. But he stepped off the stairs first, and held out his hand to help her. Feeling distinctly light-headed from sleep deprivation, she found his strong grasp oddly reassuring.

To her surprise he kept hold of it as he led her

out of the small station to a truck parked along the road. It wasn't anything like the black sedan from the palazzo she'd ridden in last night.

Heavens—was it only last night? Ally felt all mixed up and confused. She had to be confused to be happy this enigmatic stranger had rescued her from that awful train.

"Where are you taking me?" she asked once he'd turned on the engine.

"To a place where you can eat and sleep in that order."

That sounded so wonderful, she wanted to cry.

"Why would you do that for me when you had me jailed for false credentials, trespassing and impersonating someone else?" her voice trembled.

His hands tightened on the steering wheel. She could tell because his knuckles went white.

"I've found out you're who you said you were."

She jerked her head away from him so he wouldn't see her eyes smarting.

"You mean you now believe I'm Mrs. Parker…"

"Yes."

"I see. So now that you know my name, what does Mr. Montefalco call *you*?"

There was a curious silence, then, "Gino."

She stirred restlessly in the seat.

"Which may or may not be your real name, but at least it's something to call you."

"Besides bastard you mean?" he interjected in a wry tone.

Caught off guard, Ally laughed softly. She couldn't help it.

"Actually that's what I felt like calling the guard when he wouldn't help me with my suitcase on the train. Even at your worst, you were more of a gentleman."

She heard him draw in what sounded like a tortured breath. "I owe you an apology."

She flicked him a covert glance. "If I ever get to meet your employer, I'll be able to vouch for your fierce loyalty to him. It's no wonder he keeps you on his payroll. Every man who's a target should have such a trusted bodyguard."

By now they'd left the little village of Remo and were driving through fields of sunflowers with a hot Italian sun shining down.

"How do you know so much about him?"

She studied her hands. "I know very little apart from the obvious facts."

"Which are?" he prodded.

"He's rich, titled and has lost his wife. If he loved her desperately, then my heart goes out to him."

"What about your heart?" he whispered.

"If you're asking if it was shattered by my husband's death, then yes." *If you're wondering if his probable infidelity has wounded me, then yes.* But because she'd waited too long to try to fix what was wrong between them, Jim's unexpected death had brought on guilt she couldn't seem to throw off.

Gino drove along the maze of country roads with what appeared to be long accustomed practice and expertise.

Once upon a time she would have loved traveling through the countryside, but right now she was numb to the world around her.

The next time he stopped, her bleary eyes took in a yellowed, three-story farmhouse that looked quite ancient.

"Where are we?"

"My home," he announced before helping her from the car.

He carried her suitcase and told her to follow him. She didn't question him as they entered the foyer and climbed some stairs to the next floor.

He opened a door on his left. "You'll be comfortable in here, Mrs. Parker. The en suite bathroom is through that door. I'll ask my housekeeper Bianca to bring you a tray. Sleep well. We'll talk later."

"Yes, we will. I'd like my husband's laptop back."

"All in good time."

As she was coming to find out, it was his favorite saying.

He placed her suitcase on the aged hardwood floor, then left and shut the door behind him.

Straight ahead of her was a four-poster double bed with a comfy looking white quilt. She was so tired, she removed her outer clothes and climbed under the covers. Ally didn't remember her head touching the pillow.

CHAPTER THREE

ON GINO'S way down to the kitchen, Sofia met him in the dining room. "Who's that lady you brought home with you, Uncle Gino?"

Gino had to think fast. "An acquaintance of mine who wanted to see the farm. She's flown all the way from the States, and is so tired, I told her to sleep before I introduced her to you."

"Oh."

"Where's Bianca?"

"Out on the back terrace with Luigi and papa."

That was just as well. He tousled Sofia's hair. "Our guest needs food. Do you want to help me fix it?"

"Yes."

She started walking to the kitchen with him.

"What does she like?"

"Can you imagine her not liking anything Bianca cooks?"

"I guess not."

His morose niece needed her friends. Now that he was home, he would arrange for it. Together they made a plate of ham, fresh bread, salad, fruit and hot tea.

"Can I go with you to take it to her?"

"Of course."

"What's her name?"

"Signora Parker."

"Does she speak Italian?"

"No." Not according to the taxi driver. "It will give you a chance to practice your excellent English with her."

"Is she a farmer, too?"

Gino was equally curious about the wife of Donata's lover. "Why don't you ask her later?" It would be interesting to hear her answer.

They went up the stairs. He tapped on the door. *"Signora?"*

"I'll peek," Sofia offered and opened the door a crack. After tiptoeing inside, she came back out again.

"She's sound asleep."

Gino wasn't surprised. "We'll fix her another plate later."

Once back in the kitchen, they worked together to clean things up while he devoured the meal meant for the intriguing woman sleeping beneath his roof.

"She has pretty hair. It looks like the color of fairy wings."

That was as good a description of gossamer as you could get. He eyed his brunette niece he loved.

"Not many people we know have hair that particular shade do they?"

"I don't know any," she declared.

Neither did Gino.

"What do you say we call Anna's mother and see if your friend can stay over with us for a few days."

"She likes me to play at her house."

He frowned. "Why not at yours?"

"I don't know."

He put a hand on her shoulder. "I think you do. Tell me what's wrong?"

Her eyes filled with tears. "I think she's scared of Papa."

Pain shot through him. "Did she tell you that?"

"No. But the last time she came to the palazzo, Papa suddenly started walking around the rooms. He kept doing it over and over again, and—" Sofia couldn't finish.

Gino crushed her in his arms, absorbing her sobs while he let her cry her heart out. Deep inside he cried with her to think of the brother he idolized reduced to this state so early in his life. But even worse, to realize Sofia had been robbed of a normal childhood. God give him the strength to help his precious niece find some happiness before her childhood was gone.

"Would you like me to drive you to Anna's?"

"No. I don't want to go anywhere. I just want to stay with you."

That's what Gino had been afraid of. Sofia was crawling deeper and deeper inside her impenetrable shell. It was up to Gino not to let that happen. But how to prevent it when he was having trouble enough holding body and soul together?

When Ally first woke up, it took a minute for her to remember where she was.

She checked her watch. It was almost 8:00 p.m. She'd slept nine hours!

Someone must have just come in the room and brought her a tray of food. She was so grateful, and so ravenous, she ate every crumb, then drained the cup of hot tea in one go.

Her suitcase was still where Gino had left it. She carried it to the bed and got out clean clothes before hurrying into the bathroom to shower.

When she walked in the bedroom ten minutes later freshly shampooed and dressed in a clean pair of jeans and a blue cotton top, she felt a little more human again.

Delighted with her cheerful yellow room, she opened the green shutters to look outside. In the twilight she could see fields of flowers under cultivation. Incredible.

After brushing her damp hair until it formed

natural curls, she applied lipstick, then left the room and went downstairs in search of her host.

A tall, slender girl about eleven or twelve with long brown hair and large, sad brown eyes met her at the bottom of the stairs. Gino's daughter?

Ally slowed down. Of course he would have a family. Why would she even question it?

"Hello."

"Hello, Mrs. Parker," the girl said.

Ally was charmed by her manners. "What's your name?"

"Sofia."

"I *love* it."

"You do?"

"Yes. There was once a very important queen ahead of her time with that name."

The girl eyed her solemnly. "What's yours?"

"It's Ally. But I like yours much better."

"What does your name mean?"

"I don't think it means anything, but I got teased a lot because of it."

"How come?"

"Do you know what a cat is?"

"Yes. Uncle Gino got me one a couple of months ago. It's black with white feet."

Uncle Gino. That explained the superficial likeness to him.

"Lucky you. What's its name?"

"Rudolfo."

"That sounds quite magnificent."

"It's Uncle Gino's real name."

How apropos. He more than fulfilled the expectation of such a name.

"I see. Well, in my case the kids called me 'alley cat'."

"What's that?"

"A cat that lives on the streets because it doesn't have a home."

"But you had a home." She sounded worried.

"Yes, darling." The endearment just slipped out. There was a wistfulness about the girl that caught at Ally's heart strings.

"Where do you live in America?"

"Portland, Oregon. Have you heard of it?"

"I think so. Uncle Gino said you came to see his farm. Are you a farmer?"

That was as good an explanation as any for Ally's presence in the home of Mr. Montefalco's bodyguard.

"Not exactly, Sofia. But my grandparents used to have a small farm at the base of Mount Hood in Oregon. It's an old volcano."

"We have volcanoes here," Sofia confided.

"I know. Very famous ones. Someday I'd like to see them."

"Is the one by your grandparents' alive?"

"I guess they can all come alive, but Mount

Hood has been quiet for many years. The soil is perfect for growing lavender.

"That's one of the flowers Uncle Gino grows."

"I noticed. That's the reason I stopped by. The flower fields reminded me that my grandmother used to keep a garden and would give lavender away for gifts. One of my favorite memories was helping her separate it into bundles."

"I wish I could do that."

"Don't you get to help your aunt and uncle on the farm?"

"Uncle Gino's not married. He says girlfriends are much better."

At least Gino was honest. Bluntly so.

Having witnessed several sides of him already, she couldn't say she was surprised by his philosophy. It reminded her of her mother's attitude about handsome men making bad husbands. Maybe Gino and her mother had the right answer after all.

Ally moved closer. "Since you're family, I bet Gino would give you a special farm job to do if you asked him."

"Maybe I will." Sofia looked up at Ally with fresh interest. Do you want to meet my father? He hasn't gone to bed yet."

"I'd love to. What's his name?"

"Marcello."

"That's another wonderful name. What's your mother's?"

Her face closed up. "Donata."

Donata?

But that meant—that meant—

Fresh pain knifed through Ally.

Dear God—

Just then Gino emerged from the shadows of the corridor.

Ally wondered how long he'd been standing there. How much had he heard of her conversation with Sofia?

Their eyes met for an instant. As he hugged his niece to his side, she registered anguish in those black depths.

Ally leaned over and grasped the girl's hands.

"Gino told me about your mother, Sofia. I'm so sorry." Her voice shook.

I despise you, Jim Parker, for your part in depriving this child of her mother.

How was it possible Donata hadn't cherished her daughter and husband enough that she would go on vacation to Switzerland without them? It made reason stare and brought a different kind of ache to Ally's heart.

She had to clear her throat before she could speak again.

"My father died a few years ago. No matter how young or old you are, I know how much it hurts."

What had hurt Ally was to learn that her father had passed away, and she'd never once met him.

Tears trickled down the girl's pale cheeks. "Uncle Gino says I have to wait until I go to heaven to see her again."

Over the last four months Ally had thought she'd cried all the tears inside her. But in the face of seeing this child's suffering, she could feel new ones threatening.

"You and your father are going to need each other more than ever. Where is he?"

"In the kitchen with Luigi drinking his tea."

"Is Luigi your brother?"

"No. I don't have any brothers or sisters. Luigi is one of the nurses who takes care of papa."

Takes care of him?

Ally darted Gino another questioning glance. She discovered a mixture of sorrow and bleakness.

"My brother was diagnosed with Alzheimer's two years ago. His was a very rare case because it hit so hard and fast."

Ally gasped. There'd been too many painful revelations at once.

She cupped Sofia's wet cheeks. "I'd love to be introduced to your father. Can he talk at all?"

"No, but sometimes he squeezes my hand. Come with me."

She grasped one of Ally's hands and led her through the spacious dining room off the foyer to the kitchen. Ally was aware of Gino's hard-muscled body following them at a short distance.

One glimpse of the black-haired fiftyish looking man seated at the oak table, and she saw the strong resemblance between the two brothers.

As they drew closer, she noticed that Sofia had inherited her father's brown eyes and widow's peak.

Two immensely attractive men in one family. How tragic that one of them had to be stricken in the prime of life.

His attentive nurse, an auburn-haired man who looked to be in his mid-thirties like Gino, kept his patient perfectly groomed.

The Duc Di Montefalco was dressed in an elegant robe and slippers, quietly drinking tea from a mug. Sofia's cat did a big stretch at the base of his chair, as if letting Ally know he was guarding Sofia's father, so be warned.

The girl drew Ally over to him.

"Papa? This is Mrs. Parker from America."

Her father took no notice. He just kept taking sips of the hot liquid.

It killed Ally to realize that this darling girl wouldn't be able to derive the kind of love and comfort she needed from her father.

The moment was so emotional for Ally, she let go of Sofia's hand long enough to clasp Marcello's arm for a brief moment.

"How do you do, Mr. Montefalco. It's an honor to meet you," she said in a tremulous voice.

Luigi smiled. "He's very happy to meet you too, *signora*. Isn't that right, Sofia."

"Yes. He likes company."

The nurse placed a hand on Sofia's shoulder. "Do you want to help me put him to bed? I think he's still tired after our big day yesterday."

"I know he is. His eyelids are drooping." Sofia sounded way too adult for a girl her age.

Ally watched Gino kiss his niece on the cheek. "While you say good night to him, I'll be outside with Mrs. Parker. Come and find us when you're through."

"I will."

By tacit agreement Ally left the kitchen with the man she no longer thought of as her captor. Thankful he'd suggested going outside, she stepped over the threshold into the warm, fragrant night where she could breathe in fortifying gulps of air.

Gino watched her through veiled eyes. She met his glance. "Why was yesterday especially tiring for your brother?"

His features took on a hardened cast.

"The priest conducted funeral services for Donata at the church. I don't know if Marcello had any comprehension of what was going on, but Sofia insisted he did."

A sob got trapped in Ally's throat. "She's had too much grief to deal with."

"Tell me about it," he ground out. "Sofia needs her father."

Just then she heard the agony in his voice and sensed he was grieving for the loss of his brother. Any man in Gino's position would be feeling overwhelmed right now. But as she was coming to find out, Gino was no ordinary man. He had strengths she admired more than he would ever know.

Tears glazed her eyes, moistening her silky lashes. "Throughout my life I've been able to forgive those who've hurt me. But for my husband and Donata to have hurt an innocent child... Right now I'm *really* struggling."

He moved closer. "Donata was far too concerned for herself to ever consider other people's feelings, least of all her daughter's."

Ally bit her lip, realizing this man was carrying an extra heavy load now that Sofia didn't have a mother.

"I was an only child. I would have loved a sister or brother."

"Marcello and I were best friends," he whispered. "To protect him and Sofia, I've brought them to the farm where I have heavy security in place around the clock. We're safe here. No one gets in or out without my knowing about it. When the news of Donata's death is publicized, the media's going to turn it into the scandal of the decade."

Ally shuddered. Her thoughts flashed back to the night she'd spent at the jail because he'd thought she was a journalist.

"Has it always been this terrible for you?"

He nodded grimly. "Since my brother and I were old enough to go out in public with our parents, the paparazzi has dogged us. The only time I found peace or anonymity was to escape to the countryside.

"When I was away at college in England where Marcello had attended, I couldn't even look at another woman without some salacious headline showing up in the paper the next day. My every move was cataloged. The European press billed me the playboy of the decade. Perhaps some of it was deserved, but not all…

"After graduation I knew I had to end the nightmare or go a little mad. About that time tragedy struck when our parents were killed in a light plane accident.

"Marcello inherited the title, and I was left free to become a flower farmer, something I'd always wanted to do with my mother's blessing.

"So I bought property and this farmhouse. Instead of going by the name Rudolfo Di Montefalco, I became Gino Fioretto, It's an old family name on my mother's side. Until my brother became ill, I was able to live in relative obscurity. But with Donata's disappearance and death, all hell has broken loose. I moved Marcello and Sofia out of the palazzo as fast as possible.

"You'll notice I don't have TV, radio or newspapers here."

"I don't blame you—" she cried out. "If Sofia had any idea…"

Gino studied her horrified expression. "Then we understand each other?"

"Of course."

"You forgive me for my callous treatment of you at the jail?"

"Under the circumstances, I don't know how you kept any control at all."

As she lifted her tortured gaze to him, they heard Sofia call out, "Uncle Gino?"

"We're by the fountain."

Sofia came running to her uncle. He swept her up in his powerful arms.

Ally could hear Sofia denying that she was tired. It was understandable the girl didn't want to go to bed. She was in too much pain and needed her uncle. Gino was the girl's sole source of love and safety now. They needed time to themselves.

"Gino?" Ally said. "Before it gets any later, I need to make a phone call. If you two will excuse me?"

"By all means." His sober mood hadn't altered. She smiled at his niece to break the tension the girl must be sensing. "Good night, Sofia. I'm very happy to have met you."

"Me, too. You're not going away yet are you?" The question was so unexpected, it caught Ally off guard.

"Of course she isn't," Gino answered before she could, sounding the absolute authority. "She's here to tour the farm. That could take some time."

Ally trembled at the inferred warning that she shouldn't be planning to leave anytime soon.

"Can I come with you tomorrow?" The girl's brown eyes implored him.

"The three of us will do it together," Gino declared as if it were already a fait accompli.

"Maybe we could take Papa, too?" Sofia added.

"I'm sure your father would love it," Ally stated before Gino could say anything else. "Even if he can't talk, deep inside I'm sure he'll enjoy getting out in the sunshine with his beautiful daughter."

"I'm not beautiful."

Ally winked at her. "Then you haven't looked in a mirror lately." She kissed her cheek.

"Good night," she whispered before hurrying across the courtyard to the farmhouse entrance, away from Gino's enigmatic gaze.

Once she reached her room, she picked up the receiver of the house phone and made a credit card call to her mother.

"Mom?"

"Ally, honey— The caller ID said this was an out of area call. I was hoping it was you."

"Forgive me for phoning this early. Did I waken you or Aunt Edna?"

Ally's mother had been helping her widowed sister who'd come home from the hospital with a hip replacement.

"Heavens no. Edna and I have already had breakfast."

"That's good."

"How's the headache by now?"

"It's gone." As for Ally's emotional state, that was another matter entirely.

"Where are you and your friends staying?"

Ally bowed her head. It was time to tell the truth.

"That's what I'm phoning you about. I decided to take the doctor's advice and get away for a while by myself."

"I hate the thought of you being alone. Have you cleared it with the maestro?"

"I didn't need to. We have the month of June off, remember?"

"Of course. So where are you?"

"I'm staying at a bed and breakfast on a lavender farm."

"You always did love it at Mom and Dad's. I wish they were still alive so we could all be together."

"So do I, Mom."

"I'm sure the change will do you good. Where is it exactly?"

Her hand tightened on the cord. "In Italy, not far from Rome.

"Mom—" Ally spoke before her mother's shock translated into words. "Let me explain. Detective Davis told me the woman who died with Jim has been identified. She was Italian, so I flew to Switzerland, and now I'm in Italy to talk to the authorities."

"Oh, honey, you must be in terrible pain."

Ally had been in excruciating pain for months, but right now another emotion dominated her feelings. The compassion she felt for Gino and Sofia superseded all else.

"I need closure. This seems to be the best way to achieve it."

To prevent her mother from asking the burning question about Jim's involvement with Donata, Ally said, "This shouldn't take too long."

"I hope not. When you get back we'll find you another place to live that doesn't remind you of Jim."

No matter where Ally lived, she would always be haunted by two people's treachery to an innocent Italian girl who only asked to be loved.

"Mom? Will you do me a favor and call Carol? Since I couldn't make the concert because of my headache, she still has my violin. Tell her to keep it until I get back."

"I'll do better than that. Edna and I will drive over to her house and get it."

"Thank you. Please give Aunt Edna my love. I promise to keep you posted and I'll call you soon."

She hung up before her mother asked for a phone number where Ally could be reached in case of an emergency. That was the way Ally wanted it right now.

Too restless to sit still, she wandered over to the open window and looked out. If Gino and his niece were still walking, she couldn't see them.

"Signora Parker?"

At the sound of Gino's low male voice, she whirled around to discover him in the aperture. By now she ought to be used to him appearing as silently as a cat.

"I—I didn't realize you were there." Her voice caught.

"I knocked, but you were deep in thought."

So she was…

"Has Sofia gone to her room?"

"No. To her father's. If it's her only comfort right now, I'm not about to deny her. But as she's expecting me to join them, I'll say good night."

Ally had seen Gino at his most forbidding. But his tenderness toward his brother and niece revealed a side of him she found rather exceptional.

"Thank you for your hospitality, Gino. When I came to Italy, I had no idea I would end up here. Please know you can trust me with what you've told me."

"If I didn't, you'd be back in Portland right now," he ground out. "Sleep well."

He studied her for an overly long moment before disappearing.

Part of her wanted to call him back and ask him to return the laptop. If he had an adaptor, then she could see the pictures and read any e-mails Jim hadn't planned on her knowing about. But another part resisted because she knew Gino had too much on his mind to deal with anything else tonight. They'd only buried Donata yesterday. Tomorrow would be soon enough to ask for her property back.

This family needed sleep to help assuage their deep sorrow. As for Ally, she turned once more to the open window. After sleeping all day, she was wide-awake.

A slight breeze carrying a divine fragrance ruffled her curls. She rested her head against the frame, feeling herself suspended in a kind of limbo. It was almost as if she was standing outside herself, not belonging in the past or in an unknown future, but somewhere in between—a flowered fantasyland where she felt the unconditional love of one man for his family. In light of the tragedies that had befallen the Montefalco clan, Gino's devotion to those he loved touched her so deeply, she couldn't put it in words.

She finally went to bed with her mind full of new images. No matter the setting or situation, they all contained Gino...

"Where's Signora Parker?" Sofia asked Gino without even saying good morning. "We've been waiting for her."

For Sofia to be interested in a stranger she'd only met for a few minutes last night, it meant that Signora Parker had made a strong impression on his niece. It wasn't that surprising since Gino couldn't seem to put the American woman out of his mind, either.

He kissed her forehead. "I guess she's still asleep."

"But she slept all day yesterday."

Gino had a hunch Jim Parker's widow had lain awake most of the night just like Gino, and hadn't fallen asleep until dawn.

He knew she'd already had several months to grieve deeply, but he feared she could be in mourning for a long time to come. Why that knowledge bothered him he couldn't answer yet. He only knew that it did.

"I'll go upstairs and see if she's awake."

Before Gino could blink, Sofia ran out of the kitchen. His first inclination was to stop his niece from bothering their guest. But since he, too, had been looking forward to spending the day with her, he decided he was glad Sofia had taken the initiative.

In a few seconds his niece came running back. Her anxious expression disturbed him. "She's not in her room! I thought she came to see the farm. We were going to go around it together. Where did she go, Uncle Gino?"

The alarm in her voice echoed inside him.

He turned to Bianca who was pouring coffee into Marcello's cup. "Have you seen Signora Parker this morning?"

"No. Maybe she's outside taking a walk."

Gino jumped up from his chair. "I'll go look for her."

"I'll come with you," Sofia cried.

No sooner had they left through the side door off the kitchen than they spotted her in the distance. She was leaning over one of the rows in the special herb garden he'd grown expressly for Bianca.

It pleased Gino no end that she appeared to be intrigued by the various plants.

Sofia ran over to her. Ally raised a smiling face to his niece and put out an arm to hug her. The spontaneous gesture came naturally to her. She had a warmth that drew Sofia like a bee to the flowers growing on his farm.

"Good morning, *signora*."

Their eyes met. Hers shimmered like green jewels.

"This garden is fabulous, Gino."

"He made it for Bianca," Sofia exclaimed. "She likes everything fresh."

"Well isn't she lucky that the owner of this farm appreciates her so much."

He chuckled. "I'm the lucky one. You'll see why when you eat one of her meals."

"I'm looking forward to it."

"Come on, Ally. She has breakfast ready for us."

"I'm coming."

Gino watched her straighten. Dressed in a skirt and a peach top her curvaceous figure did wonders for, Gino found himself staring at her.

Hopefully his niece was oblivious as she pulled their lovely houseguest along. Gino hardly recognized Sofia in light of her affection for Ally whom she was already treating like an old friend.

A minute later they were all assembled at the table with Bianca fussing over them.

"I tell you what, Sofia," Gino spoke up. "On our ride we'll drop by the Rossinis'. You've never met my farm manager, Dizo. He and his wife Maria have two daughters. One of them, Leonora, is your exact age. She's a very nice girl who has been asking to meet you. You'll like her."

"Do we have to do that today? I just want to be with you and Ally."

His niece was transparent. For months she'd been so unhappy, he'd been at a loss how to help her. Now suddenly Ally Parker had come into their lives. When was the last time any of them had experienced any happiness?

Gino had to think back twelve years when both brothers had been in their prime, their parents had still been alive and all was well with their world. Until the advent of Donata...

He peeled an orange and gave a couple of sections to Marcello who automatically ate them. Gino was still incredulous that his brother would never be normal again, would never be able to make his daughter laugh and feel secure again.

In the past Marcello could always make things right for Sofia no matter how her mother neglected her. Everyone loved Marcello, especially Gino.

Sometimes like now, the pain of loss was unbearable. He could only imagine how much his niece suffered. Yet this morning she wasn't showing any signs of heartache.

"Tell you what, Sofia. I'll run over to the Rossinis' to check on business, then come back and we'll all go swimming at the river. How does that sound?"

Ally was bent over her food and didn't make eye contact with him.

"I can't wait! Don't take too long, Uncle Gino."

Maybe Leonora would return with him so the girls could meet. He left the kitchen and went outside to start up the truck.

A few minutes later he pulled to a stop in the parking area surrounding the covered stands. The usual crowd of customers kept the staff busy. He looked around to see if Leonora was helping her mother.

Maria was in charge of the workers who ran Gino's flower market called Fioretto's. What wasn't shipped from his farm to different areas of the country by train and a fleet of trucks was sold as overflow to the local businesses who sent their buyers to his farm.

Several of the staff recognized him and waved. He reciprocated as he moved past basket after basket of flowers that would all be sold by three in the afternoon.

"Ah, Gino— Over here!" Maria called to him. She was surrounded by customers. Once she was free they talked business for a few minutes.

"Is there anything I can do for you before you go?" she asked at last.

"I need two bunches of lavender."

"Coming up." She wrapped them in paper and handed them to him. "Is Leonora around?"

"No. She's home tending the baby who has a cold."

"I was hoping she could come over and meet my niece."

Maria's eyes rounded. "She would love it! Maybe tomorrow. I could ask Dizo to drive her."

"That would be fine, Maria. I'll arrange to have her driven back later in the day. *Ciao*."

"*Ciao*, Gino."

He hurried out to his truck anxious to get back to the farmhouse. To Ally. Since finding her in the herb garden this morning, he was still so mesmerized by her femininity and shapely figure, he almost climbed into the cab of another truck before he realized what he was doing.

In point of fact, Ally Parker shouldn't be here. She shouldn't be anywhere in Italy where the paparazzi could find her. Carlo would have a coronary if he knew. But Gino couldn't think about that right now.

She was here under his roof. That's where he wanted her to stay.

He'd admired the fight she'd put up at the jail. She never once acted like a victim. Signora Parker had fire and guts, the kind you didn't often see in a man or a woman.

Jim Parker hadn't deserved a wife like her any more than Marcello had deserved Donata…

Gino gritted his teeth to think of the pain

Donata had caused, but by the time he returned to the farm and saw Ally out in front with Sofia, his dark thoughts evaporated.

No sooner did he stop his truck than they walked up to him. He jumped down and handed them their gifts.

"What's this?" Ally stared at him.

"Open it and find out."

Sofia actually giggled in delight. Gino put a hand on her arm. "Why don't you take yours inside and open it with your father?"

"I will! Thank you, Uncle Gino." She kissed his cheek, then ran across the courtyard to the house.

The woman at his side was busy opening hers. "Oh, Gino— Fresh lavender. It's wonderful!"

"So are you."

She quickly lowered her eyes as a subtle blush filled her cheeks.

"Your presence has made Sofia happy. She needs people around who care about her. An outing with you is exactly what the doctor ordered."

"No child should have to live through a nightmare like this."

"I agree, Signora Parker. That's why I'm indebted to you for staying with us."

"Please don't keep calling me Signora Parker. It makes me feel old. My name is Ally."

"I've thought of you as Ally for quite a while, but was waiting for your permission to use it."

She finally looked up at him. "Well you have it. If you'll excuse me, I'll just run these flowers in the house, then come right back."

She took a few steps then paused. "I'm afraid I didn't bring a swimsuit with me."

"No problem. I'll run you and Sofia into Remo to shop. After Sofia's growth spurt this last year, she needs a new one."

"All right. Then I'll see you in a minute."

"*Bene.*" The Italian word slipped out of his mouth as he watched her walk away carrying the lavender in the crook of her arm. Like a bride approaching the altar with her sheaf…

Once again he was struck by how incredibly attractive she was. If he were her husband…

CHAPTER FOUR

WITH her heart pounding, Ally found Bianca and asked her to get a vase for the flowers she could take to her room.

The unexpected gift had whipped up her sense of excitement which was way out of proportion to the situation. The reason being that Gino was an incredible man.

Her friend Carol would call him drop dead gorgeous.

He was. But he was a lot more than that.

He had character and nobility along with those striking looks. Somehow Ally needed to forget what the combination was doing to her, how he made her feel when they were together.

Something was wrong with her to have these feelings over a man she barely knew when she'd only come here to talk to Donata's husband. It didn't make sense. She needed to get her head on straight.

But the second she walked back outside with

Sofia and felt Gino's eyes assessing her with an intimacy that made her legs go weak, she realized she was in serious trouble.

His niece ran up to him. "Papa loves the lavender. He just keeps smelling it. Bianca loves it, too. She says it's been too long since there were fresh flowers in the house."

Ally shot Gino a teasing glance. "And you, a flower farmer. Shame on you."

He broke into a full-bodied smile, turning him into the most attractive man she'd ever seen in her life. The European tabloids must have made a fortune just following him around snapping pictures.

Her heart kept rolling over on itself.

"Mea culpa. It takes a woman to civilize a man's abode."

"What's an abode, Uncle Gino?"

"A house. Come on. Up you go." He'd opened the truck door to help her inside.

Ally had purposely waited so she wouldn't have to sit next to him. But by making that decision, she'd left herself open to more scrutiny while he assisted her.

Careful to keep her skirt from riding up her thigh, she climbed in, aware of his appraising glance as she swung her legs to the floor. He seemed to pause before shutting the door.

When he finally walked around and got in

behind the wheel, she exhaled the breath she'd been holding.

"Bianca has packed us a picnic lunch and some towels," he informed them. "Paolo will bring everything when he drives Luigi and Marcello to the river."

Ally eyed the girl seated next to her.

"Do you like to swim, Sofia?"

"I used to when Papa swam with me at the palazzo."

Gino's gaze met Ally's with the implicit message that his niece gauged all her happiness before Marcello had been afflicted.

Ally had no words. All she could do was put her arm around Sofia and pull her close.

An hour later while Gino and Luigi helped Marcello swim, Ally and Sofia sat huddled in huge beach towels beneath a shade tree to watch.

The river was more like a stream that broadened in parts. Near the tree it was deep enough to come up to Ally's neck. On such a hot day, the refreshing water couldn't have been more welcome.

Thankful Gino had been too occupied helping his brother to pay much attention to Ally, she and Sofia had played in the water for a while. When Ally thought it was safe from Gino's all-seeing glance she'd scrambled out, but not before he'd caught her attempting to cover her bikini clad figure with the towel. Warmth still filled her cheeks, the kind she couldn't blame on the sun.

Sofia sat next to her, eating a roll and cheese.

"I think your father is enjoying himself, don't you?"

Sofia nodded. "I wish Uncle Gino could be with us all the time, but I know he can't. He has to do Papa's business and run the farm, too."

"That's too much for any man," Ally declared. She munched on a ripe plum and looked all around them. "This is a heavenly place. I could stay here forever."

"I love it, too! But Mama would never let me come."

"Why not?"

"She said she didn't think Uncle Gino liked her very much so she preferred I stay at the palazzo. I told her Uncle Gino liked everyone and was my favorite person next to her and Papa. But she wouldn't talk about it."

Ally moaned inwardly. "Maybe your mama was a city girl."

Sofia looked at her. "Are you a city girl?"

"I like the city, but to be honest, I preferred my grandparents' farm. Unfortunately when they died, my mother and her older sister sold it so they would have money to live."

"Why didn't you all just live there?"

"Because Aunt Edna got married, and my

mother was divorced. She had to raise me on her own, and she didn't like farming."

"What *did* she like?"

"Her talent was music. She could play the piano so well she gave lessons. It would have been hard to find enough students in the country, so we lived in Portland."

"Did she teach you to play?"

"Yes. Do you play an instrument?"

"I started the piano, but I wasn't very good and quit."

Ally chuckled. "I didn't like it, either, but my mother said I had to learn to play something, so I started on the violin."

"Did you like it?"

"I loved it so much, I play in the Portland symphony orchestra. It's how I earn my living, but right now the orchestra is on vacation, so I decided to come here for a holiday."

It wasn't a complete lie.

Sofia's eyes lit up. "I've been to the symphony a lot with my papa and Gino. Do you have to wear black?"

"On performance night, yes."

The girl sighed. "I wish I were good at something."

"I'm sure you're good at a lot of things. You just haven't discovered all of them yet. My husband hated piano lessons but he became an expert skier."

The observation had just slipped out.

Sofia studied her for a moment. "How come he didn't come with you?"

The question Ally had been waiting for…

"He died a while ago."

The girl looked wounded. "Do you have children?"

A pain seared Ally. "We weren't married long enough for that to happen. I always wanted a son or a daughter like you. But I have my mother and aunt, and you have your father and your uncle."

Sofia sighed. "I'm glad they're both alive."

"You're very lucky to have them."

"After we tour the farm, do you want to see where my mother is buried?"

"If you'd like me to."

"We don't have a headstone yet. Uncle Gino told me I should decide what to have engraved on it since I'm the Duchess Di Montefalco now. But I don't know what to put."

A duchess at eleven years of age. So much responsibility for a young girl. What Jim would have given…

On Ally's honeymoon he'd admitted wanting more from life than a stable job with a steady income. She heard his resentment when he spoke of people who'd been born to a life of privilege and wealth, and he hadn't.

She'd thought he was like most people who

had their dream of winning the lottery or something, so she didn't place any stock in it. But over time Jim began to change into someone restless and ambitious. Before long he was willing to spend more and more time apart from her in order to get financially ahead, as he put it.

That *did* alarm her since she'd wanted to start a family.

The marriage that should have lasted a lifetime began to fall apart. Though she'd longed to have a baby, knowing what she knew now, Ally was thankful it hadn't happened.

She glanced at Gino's niece, feeling a bond with her that made her want to protect her every bit as fiercely as Gino did.

"Do you happen to know your mother's full name?"

"Yes. It's Donata Ricci-Cagliostro Di Montefalco."

"What a beautiful name. Since you know it you could say 'In memory of our beloved wife and mother,' then put her full name, and the dates."

Sofia pondered the suggestion for a minute. "I think that's perfect. I'm going to tell Uncle Gino right now."

She threw off her towel and ran toward the edge of the river where the men were just getting out.

The girl's voice carried in the light breeze.

Gino drew closer to the picnic blanket. His black eyes sought Ally's with such impact, she could hardly breathe.

"What do you girls say we go back to the farmhouse to change, then I'll drive you and Sofia around the farm."

Bemused by his unexpected aura of contentment and his blatant masculine appeal, Ally averted her eyes. The sight of Gino was too much. He put the sun god Apollo to shame.

"Let me gather up the remains of this delicious picnic first."

The rest of the afternoon turned out to be magical.

Dressed in jeans and T-shirts, Ally and Sofia rode in the back of Gino's truck. To Sofia's delight, he drove them through the colorful flower fields where they waved at the workers. She wondered which ones were the security guards Gino had posted to watch over his domain.

At different times he pulled to a stop and the three of them walked on the rich earth enjoying the fragrant air beneath a sunny sky.

A last stop at the cemetery to put some fresh flowers on Donata's grave, and they drove back to the farmhouse for dinner.

"Can we do this again tomorrow?" Sofia pled with Gino.

"Tomorrow I've arranged for Leonora to come over."

"But I don't know her. I'd rather be with you and Ally."

Gino patted her hand. "I have to do some work tomorrow, sweetheart."

Ally decided the two of them needed to be alone. While they'd been driving around, she realized it was time to separate herself from Gino and Sofia who, like her uncle, had already become too important to her.

Without hesitation Ally got up from the table. "If you will excuse me, I have to go upstairs and pack."

Two pairs of eyes swerved to hers in an instant. Sofia's were already full of tears. Gino's expression bordered on anger.

"I wasn't aware you were leaving to go anywhere," he muttered with barely concealed impatience.

"I put off my flight a day in order to spend it with you. Now that I've toured your farm, I—I have to return to Rome first thing in the morning," she stammered. "My flight to Portland leaves in the afternoon."

She hurried out of the kitchen and headed for the guest room upstairs. Ally couldn't stay here any longer. Today there'd been moments when it had felt like the three of them were a family. Sofia had already endeared herself to Ally. As for Gino…

With every second she spent in his thrilling

company, she was losing her objectivity. To stay in Italy any longer would be playing with fire. She'd come to Italy to talk to Marcello, but his illness made that impossible. She had no excuse to stay any longer. She would only be intruding on Gino's personal life.

Ally hadn't missed Sofia's aside when the housekeeper told Gino that Merlina had dropped by the farmhouse while they'd been out.

"Merlina is one of Uncle Gino's girlfriends. Sometimes she used to come to the palazzo to talk to Mama about him." Hearing those words, Ally had actually experienced a stab of jealousy! Everything was getting far too complicated. She needed to go home and leave temptation behind. Back in Portland she would find herself another place to live. Keeping busy would prevent her from thinking too much. Fantasizing too much about impossible dreams.

To stay here any longer would be disastrous.

By the time she reached the bedroom, she heard footsteps behind her and wheeled around to discover Gino had followed her. With his rock-hard body filling the aperture, it prevented her from shutting the door. She had no choice but to back away from him.

"Earlier today," he began in a neutral tone of voice she couldn't help but envy, "Sofia and I had a conversation. Before you get carried away with plans, how would you like the job of teaching her the violin for the summer?"

Ally let out a soft cry of surprise. In the semi-darkness his eyes glowed like hot coals. "Sofia told me that's how you earn your living. I had no idea you were an accomplished violinist. She begged me to ask you to teach her the fundamentals.

"You've sparked something in my niece I didn't know was possible. I'm indebted to you, Ally, and I'll make it worth your time financially to stay here."

Ally was stunned.

More than anything in the world she wanted to say yes, but she didn't dare. Another night under his roof and she feared she'd want to stay forever, not just for a summer.

Trying to catch her breath she said, "I'm sorry, Gino, but I can't."

I can't. Don't ask me.

"I'm under contract with the symphony. We start rehearsing again in July."

His expression darkened. "You want me to tell that to a young girl downstairs who today had her first taste of happiness in over two years?"

"That's not fair—" she cried.

His black brows furrowed. "Nothing about this situation has been fair—" he bit out.

"Even so, Gino, I—"

"Even so nothing," he cut her off without

apology. "Every contract has a clause that exempts a person under extraordinary circumstances. When you explain what you've been going through, I can guarantee they'll allow you whatever time you need."

Ally knew it was true, but that wasn't what concerned her the most.

He cocked his dark head. "I don't expect you to be a babysitter, if that's what's worrying you. All I ask is that you give her an hour a day. You two can work out the time that's most convenient for you. The rest of the time you'll be free to do whatever you want.

"The farmhouse has rooms rarely used. You could choose any one of them to practice in. "You can use one of my trucks so you can drive where you want. When you don't choose to eat out, Bianca will prepare your meals."

She put up her hands. "Stop, Gino. You're making it difficult for me to refuse."

Lines marred his features. "As the acting Duc Di Montefalco, I plan to make it so damn hard, you wouldn't dare."

Acting Duc… No wonder he was given such preferential treatment everywhere he went. It explained his being able to take over at the jail as if he were in charge.

She had trouble swallowing.

"You don't understand."

"No, I don't, not after Mrs. James Parker spent a brutal night in jail insisting she needed to meet in private with the Duc Di Montefalco and no one else. That woman never once backed down.

"Your courage, like your beauty, is the talk of the Montefalco police department."

Her breathing grew shallow. "You must be talking about someone else."

"No," his voice grated. "I was there, remember? If you need reminding, take the advice you gave Sofia and look in the mirror. It will remove all doubt."

Maybe she was mistaken to think she saw a brief flash of desire in his eyes.

When she thought of the women he'd known in the past—no doubt beautiful women who'd do anything to be seen and loved by him—

All she knew was that it found an answering chord in her. She couldn't help wondering how it would feel to be kissed by him. Thoroughly kissed. Just imagining it made her so unsteady, she weaved and had to hold on to the corner of the dresser for support.

"After Leonora goes home tomorrow, I'll drive you and Sofia into town. You can pick out violins and anything else you need to get her started. Think about it. If necessary, make any phone calls you need to. Then come downstairs and give me your answer."

He disappeared too fast for her to call him back. She couldn't.

With her senses as alive as a red-hot wire, she couldn't muster a coherent thought, let alone talk.

Four months ago she couldn't have conceived of a time when she would be so attracted to another man, she would consider staying with him. Especially when she knew she was already in emotional jeopardy.

Uncle Gino prefers his girlfriends.

Such were Sofia's words.

As if thinking about the girl conjured her up, Gino's niece tapped on the open door.

"Hi," Ally said in a shaky voice.

"Hello. Is it all right if I come in?"

"Please do." Ally tried to sound normal, but it was difficult because Sofia's unexpected visit to the bedroom had thrown her.

"Did Uncle Gino tell you I'd like to take violin lessons?"

Ally nodded.

"I know this is the country, but if you gave lessons to my friend Anna, and maybe to Leonora and her sister, that would make four students. It would give you more money. I could pay for my lessons from the allowance Uncle Gino gives me."

Ally let out a heaving sigh. "It's not the money, Sofia. I—I just wouldn't feel right about staying here at your uncle's."

"You could stay at the palazzo. Nobody's there but the staff. Paolo would drive me for my lessons."

She smothered a groan. "Your uncle wants you and your father with him for the summer. He can't be worried about you going back and forth."

They couldn't risk Ally being seen by journalists just waiting for an opportunity.

Sofia studied her. "I thought you liked it here."

"I do," she rushed to assure her. More than Sofia would ever know. But—

"This is a big farmhouse," Sofia kept talking. "And Uncle Gino has to be gone a lot. He says you can stay as long as you want."

"That's very generous of him."

"He says if you agree, he's got a special surprise planned for us."

Ally could feel her defenses crumbling. "What kind of surprise?"

Suddenly Gino appeared in the doorway again looking devilishly handsome.

"You'll have to wait and see," he answered for his niece. "I promise it will be something neither of you will want to miss."

Ally had run out of excuses. With both of them imploring her to say yes, she couldn't take the pull on her heart any longer. Sofia needed love. As for Gino, she realized he needed someone to lean on. If she could help him through this transition with his niece, why not. Part of her felt she owed them.

"I tell you what. For the next few weeks I'd be happy to get you started on the violin. But when my vacation is over at the end of June, I'll have to go home."

I'll *have* to.

Gino put his hands on Sofia's shoulders. "We'll accept that arrangement, won't we, sweetheart."

Sofia was beaming. "Yes."

His eyes held a strange glitter of satisfaction. "Then let's say good night to our guest. In the morning we'll make our plans over breakfast."

"Good night, Ally," Sofia murmured. "I can't wait till tomorrow."

At this point Ally was a mass of jumbled emotions. Avoiding Gino's probing gaze she said, "I'm looking forward to it, too."

"We all are." As Gino closed the door, the silky timbre of his parting words almost caused her legs to buckle.

She'd done it now. There was no going back or it would crush Sofia. Even Ally could see the girl was fragile.

But no more so than Ally who would be worse off when she eventually left Italy. At least Sofia would still have Gino.

When Gino's cell phone went off the next morning, he was already up and shaved. Knowing Ally Parker was in his house, and wouldn't be leaving Italy anytime soon, had to be the reason he'd awakened with a sense of exhilaration he hadn't experienced in years.

He left the bathroom and went back to his room where he'd left the phone on the dresser.

He checked the caller ID, then clicked on.

"*Buon giorno*, Maria."

"*Buon giorno*, Gino."

"Is Dizo bringing Leonora, or do you want me to come and get her?"

"I'm calling because the children are sick. They've all come down with colds. Leonora is running a temperature. I'm so sorry, Gino. She's very upset that I won't let her leave the house."

"It's all right, Maria."

It was better than all right. She'd just given him the excuse to spend the morning with Ally and Sofia.

"Tell Leonora we'll look forward to seeing her when she's better. *Ciao.*"

A few minutes later he went downstairs where he could hear female voices drifting through the rooms. The animation in Sofia's chatter when she never chattered was like a balm to his soul.

The sight of their blond guest at the breakfast table dressed in a soft yellow blouse and white skirt, was more intoxicating than his first breath of fresh air when he opened his bedroom window at sunup.

Bianca had outdone herself to make an American breakfast. She buzzed around the kitchen with new energy. Marcello appeared to have a healthy appetite. His eggs and fruit juice were disappearing fast.

As Gino and Roberto, the other nurse, exchanged a silent greeting of amusement, Sofia cried, "We thought you'd never come down, Uncle Gino."

Was she speaking for their guest, too?

His gaze flicked to Ally's. Her eyes reflected a lush spring-green in the morning light coming through the windows. With glowing skin and diaphanous hair, she didn't look a day over twenty-two.

"I had a phone call from Maria," he explained taking his place at the table across from Ally. "She told me her children are sick with colds. Leonora is running a fever and can't come over today. Maybe tomorrow."

"That's okay." Sofia didn't sound at all bothered by the change in plan. "Will you take us to get our violins this morning? Then you can do your work."

Gino chuckled. So did Ally. His niece was definitely an organizer.

"I don't see why not."

Her brown eyes sparkled, another first in several years. He saw the promise of a lovely woman inside the girl who reminded him so much of Marcello, it brought a pang to his chest.

"Ally said we should rent them and practice for a few days to see if we like them first."

His gaze trapped Ally's.

"You're the expert, so we'll bow to your judgment." Anything to prevent her from changing her mind and leaving.

His good mood had made him ravenous. He ate a double helping of everything.

After he'd praised Bianca for her cooking, he suggested they get going.

On the way out to the truck, Sofia caught hold of his arm. Ally hadn't joined them yet.

"I think we should practice in the living room because there's a piano. Is that all right with you?"

"I can't think of a better place."

"Good. Did you know Ally can play the piano, too? She says when I've learned a few songs, she can accompany me."

"That doesn't surprise me a bit, sweetheart. Signora Parker is a woman of many parts."

Gino wouldn't be satisfied until he knew all of them...

CHAPTER FIVE

ALLY climbed in the truck with an eagerness she was hard-pressed to conceal. It was because of the black-haired man at the wheel. He looked fantastic this morning in a navy polo shirt and cream trousers. Ally decided that Italian men just looked better in their clothes. Of course she'd seen him at the river yesterday when all he'd been wearing were his black trunks. The truth was, he needed no embellishment.

She'd only known him a short while, but so far she could find no fault with him.

That was the scary part. She felt she was under some sort of spell.

To be recently widowed and yet this happy when she was living on borrowed time, defied logic.

They reached Remo in no time at all. "Here we are. I made inquiries and learned that Petelli's should have everything you need."

They'd pulled up alongside an arcade with shops that had been built the century before.

Sofia followed Ally out of the truck, then ran ahead to view the instruments displayed in the front window of the music store.

Ally glimpsed a guitar, harp, cello, viola and violin. She was no more immune to the sight of a beautifully crafted instrument than Sofia who grasped her arm.

"Let's go inside."

Gino held the door open for them. Ally's arm brushed against his chest as she trailed Sofia. The contact caused her to gasp softly.

Fearing Gino had heard her, she rushed over to the counter where a man probably in his late seventies smiled at them. She had a feeling he was the owner.

"Good morning," Ally greeted him. He nodded. "Do you speak English?"

"A little. Your husband can translate, *si*?"

"Yes," Gino responded, drawing up next to her.

She gave him a covert glance and noticed his eyes were smiling.

While heat crept into Ally's cheeks, Sofia said something to the man in Italian.

"Ah…she's the professor."

"Yes," Ally exclaimed. "We would like to rent two violins."

"For the little one and her father?"

Once again Sofia came to the rescue, obviously to Gino's delight because a rumble of laughter came out of him, deep and full bodied. The attractive sound reverberated through Ally's nervous system.

The owner eyed her with curiosity. "No violin for the little one's papa?"

The man was a huge tease. She couldn't help smiling at him. "No."

"*You* are the professor, and you need a violin?"

"Yes. I left mine in America."

"Are you good?"

"I try."

"*Momento.*" He turned behind him and reached in the case for one of the violins. Then he found her a bow from the drawer.

After tuning the instrument, he placed both items on the counter in front of her. "Play something by Tchaikovsky. Then I know which violin is for you."

Ally was more nervous than the time she had to audition in front of the maestro and the concert master. But her adrenaline wasn't surging because of the owner. She wanted to perform her best for Gino and his niece.

Once she'd fit the violin under her chin, she reached for the bow and began playing the final movement of Tchaikovsky's violin concerto.

Normally when Ally played, she receded into

another world. But this was one time she couldn't forget her surroundings. With Gino's black eyes riveted on her, all she could think about was him, how loving he was to Sofia, how tenderly he treated his brother. What she couldn't tell him in words, she found herself compelled to say to him through her music. She wanted to ease the pain and suffering of this wonderful, selfless man.

"Stop—stop—" the owner cried.

Ally turned to him, surprised and confused. She saw him wiping his eyes.

"Give me the violin."

Ally handed it to him. He put it back in the case, then unlocked another one.

"Here. This is a Stradivari. Now finish, please."

Whether it was an authentic Stadivarius, or a model of one copied from the master violin maker in Cremona, Italy, Ally trembled as she fit it beneath her chin and finished the Tchaikovsky.

The difference in instruments made such a difference in the sound, she could have wept for the beauty of it. When she'd come to the end, there was silence, then a burst of applause from several people who'd come into the shop without her being aware of it.

While Gino and Sofia stared at her mesmerized, the owner clapped his hands.

"Bravo, *signora*. Bravo, Bravo."

Ally handed the violin and bow back to him. "Thank you for the privilege of being allowed to play it," she said to him.

Sofia's eyes had filled.

"I'll never be able to play like you."

Ally leaned over and kissed her forehead. "You never know until you try. Once upon a time, I was just like you. I'd never even held a violin in my hand."

She raised up and looked at the owner. "Let's fit her with one her size. I'll rent the violin you first gave me to try. We'll need a music stand, and some beginner books."

Before Ally could say she would pay for her own rental, Gino gave the other man a credit card.

As they gathered up their purchases and went back out to the truck, Gino was oddly silent. For that matter, so was Sofia. That is until they arrived at the farmhouse where she glimpsed an unfamiliar car parked near the fountain.

Roberto, another nurse she'd been introduced to, was taking Marcello for a walk in the courtyard.

The second Ally climbed down so Sofia could get out, the girl ran over to show them her violin case. "Bring Papa in the house, Roberto. He's going to love hearing Ally play. He'll think he's at the symphony again!"

While Ally watched the three of them head for the front door, she heard footsteps behind her.

The next thing she knew Gino had turned her around by the shoulders.

His features solemn, he grasped both her hands and kissed her fingertips. She thought his breathing sounded labored.

"Sometimes there aren't words. Today was one of those times." His black eyes streamed into hers. "How in God's name could your husband have done what he did?"

His comment made her realize that some if not all of those pictures in the laptop were of Donata. It verified beyond any doubt that Jim had betrayed Ally. Now it meant Gino was party to her secret *and* her humiliation. Since he knew the truth, there was nothing to hide. She could be frank with him.

"That's what I ask myself about Donata every time I look into the face of her precious daughter. She's so blessed to have you to look after her and love her."

"Ally—" Gino whispered huskily before they both heard footsteps and saw Bianca hurrying toward them. Ally pulled her hands away from him in a self-conscious gesture.

The housekeeper ran up to him and said something in rapid Italian.

Though the spiel was unintelligible, Ally heard the name Merlina.

After Bianca went back to the farmhouse Gino said, "It appears I have a visitor."

"I recognized the name." The same woman had come by the day before.

Not wanting Gino to know how upset she was, Ally started for the back of the truck to get her violin.

In a few strides he'd joined her.

"How do you know about her?"

"Sofia told me she's your girlfriend."

"Was," his voice grated. "I ended it with her before Donata's disappearance."

His personal life was his own affair, yet the news set her pulse racing.

He reached in the truck bed for her instrument case and the other purchases.

"Let's go inside. While I talk to her in the study, you and Sofia can get started in the living room."

"I'll need to freshen up first." She ran ahead of him, but once again he caught up to her and held the front door open for her.

She dashed inside the foyer and up the stairs. On the way she caught sight of a lovely redheaded woman who'd come out into the hall.

Though Ally believed Gino when he said his relationship with this Merlina was over, she wished she hadn't seen her.

The presence of a former girlfriend in his house served as a wake-up call to remind Ally he preferred his single status. He could have any woman he wanted. It hardly made sense that he would be seriously interested in a twenty-eight-year-old widow who hadn't been able to keep her husband from straying.

Only one reason would bring the striking Italian woman here two days in a row. She'd come to pay her respects because she loved Gino and couldn't bear to think their relationship had ended.

It made Ally realize how futile it would be to fall in love with him.

If Ally's mother knew she'd agreed to stay with him until July, she would say her daughter was an even greater fool than before. Ally would never hear the end of it.

"It's been all over the news for the last two days," Merlina exclaimed the minute Gino ushered her back into his study. "The police are saying that the accident that killed Donata and that American man might not have been an accident. According to them the brakes might have been tampered with and you've been named their prime suspect."

Thanks to Carlo who'd phoned him night before last, Gino already knew the worst of the lies.

"It's the usual malicious propaganda put out to sell papers, Merlina. You've wasted a trip to come and tell me something I've been dealing with for a score of years now. The media will say or do anything to create a story out of nothing.

It's the way they work. If they couldn't print distortions, there would be no news anyone would want to read."

"But Gino—this time it's different because Donata was killed! Don't forget she wasn't just a local. She was the Duchess Di Montefalco."

Gino heard the envy in Merlina's voice.

"I know you could never have hurt her or anyone else. It isn't in you. But in this case you have to take this seriously."

His jaw hardened. "I don't have to do anything, Merlina."

"Please don't get angry with me. You know how I feel about you, how I've always felt. I love you, and I'm afraid for you."

"There's no need to be. This is a nine day wonder that'll pass just like all the other scandalous lies made up to try to ruin my family's happiness."

"It's so unfair to you." She pushed her hair behind her ear. "I don't have to be back in Gubbio before tomorrow. Why don't we go someplace and I'll help you get your mind off things."

He folded his arms, resting his body against the closed door. There was only one woman who could accomplish that miracle. She was living beneath his roof.

"I'm gratified by your faith in me, Merlina. Your concern means a great deal. But to take up where we left off isn't possible. Whatever we had was over a long time ago. To pretend otherwise wouldn't be fair to either of us."

Her face closed up. "What happened to your feelings for me, Gino?"

He pursed his lips. "We've been over this ground before. We shared some good times, but that's all they were."

Her eyes grew suspiciously bright. "I was hoping if I stayed away for a while, you'd be excited to see me again."

He hated to be cruel, but she was asking for it. "I'm only sorry you made this trip for nothing."

"There's someone else, isn't there."

The salvo shot straight to his gut.

"Whatever is going on in my life is my business, Merlina. If you don't mind, I have a busy day ahead of me so I'll see you out."

"Who's that blond woman who came in with you a few minutes ago?"

Gino was stunned by her aggressiveness.

"You saw the violin cases. She's a teacher who has come to help Sofia focus on something constructive."

Merlina shook her head, causing her red hair to swish. "I saw her go up the stairs. I've never heard of you allowing another woman to live in your house."

"These aren't ordinary circumstances. Sofia just buried her mother. She's grieving."

"And you actually expect me to believe this woman has nowhere else to live while she instructs your niece? Can she actually play?"

Even as she asked the mocking question, they both heard the sounds of the Tchaikovsky. Sofia must have begged Ally to play for Marcello, and she'd chosen the first movement.

Ally didn't need the Stradivari to make her violin sing. She had the touch of an angel.

Merlina looked shocked. "Who is she?"

Time to get rid of her before she learned Ally's identity.

"Someone helping Sofia find a reason to go on living."

He unfolded his arms and opened the door. "After you, Merlina."

For a minute he thought she was going to create a scene. Finally she said, "I'm leaving."

Thank God.

He walked her to the front door and watched her drive out of the courtyard.

The difference between the women he'd known and Ally was so great, the normal comparisons didn't apply.

He moved to the doorway of the living room to listen.

Roberto and Bianca were understandably awestruck. But it was Marcello who sat in the recliner, his whole body in an attitude of being spellbound. Normally nothing going on around him fazed him.

This was different. Just by the way Marcello's hands gripped the arm rests, Gino could tell how happy it made him.

The Montefalco family had been concertgoers for years. Having heard great music before, his brother's soul recognized it.

As for Sofia, she sat on the couch, entranced.

Thankful for Ally who'd managed to captivate his entire family, Gino decided this was the best time to get a little farming business done. The sooner he got things out of the way, the sooner he'd be home to spend the evening with Ally.

One of the hardest things he had to do was tear himself away when all he wanted was to get her to himself so they could concentrate on each other. His gut instinct told him that besides her affection for Sofia, Ally didn't dislike him, even if she'd only recently buried her husband. What he needed was time to prove there was an attraction between them, even if she was fighting it. Tonight couldn't come soon enough.

Ally learned that in most Italian households, the family didn't eat supper until eight or later.

At 6:20 Gino still hadn't come home. Ally had an idea it wasn't all farm business that detained him. Even if he'd ended it with Merlina months ago, the other woman lived in denial. Ally knew all about that dangerous state of mind and was living proof of her own weakness where that was concerned.

Evidently Merlina still had the same lesson to learn and had come by Gino's house to try to stir up the old spark. Ally felt a stab of pain to think maybe it hadn't been that difficult to entice Gino after all.

Thankfully Ally had a job to do teaching Sofia about the violin. There was a lot to learn first about the various parts, how to string it and tune it.

Once immersed in showing her the proper technique of using the bow, Ally was able to separate her thoughts about Gino long enough to concentrate on her delightful student.

The girl was eager to learn. Because she'd taken piano lessons, Sofia was able to read notes which was a big help. If she could maintain this enthusiasm, she would see great results.

Before Ally knew it, the day had gone. Sofia didn't want to stop. Ally chuckled and gave her a hug.

"We've done enough for one day, but I bet your father would love to see the progress you've made."

With that suggestion, the girl ran from the room with her violin and bow.

Ally took a little walk outside to stretch her muscles.

Gino's truck was parked in the courtyard, but there was no sign of him or Merlina's car.

Deciding she wasn't about to hang around waiting for him to return from wherever, she went back in the farmhouse to find the housekeeper. Bianca was in the kitchen preparing food.

"I need to go into Remo, so I won't be eating dinner. Gino said I could use one of the trucks."

The other woman nodded. "Take his. The keys are in the ignition."

"He won't mind?"

"No, no. Before he left he said you should use it if you needed to."

Gino thought of everything.

"Thank you, Bianca. If Sofia should ask, tell her I had some errands to run."

The housekeeper smiled her assent. "She's a good student, yes?"

"Very good. In another week she'll be able to play tunes for her father."

She left the house and hurried out to the truck. Glad it wasn't dark yet, Ally started it up and headed away from the farmhouse. It gave her a secret thrill to put her hands on the steering wheel where his hands had been earlier today. Everything about him thrilled her. That was the problem. She didn't want to be like Merlina who couldn't stay away from him.

Ally pressed on the accelerator. She had no

particular destination in mind. All she knew was that he wouldn't find her watching breathlessly for him when he decided to come home.

With her mind made up to be gone for a few hours, she found her way into the small town of Remo. En route she memorized certain signposts so she wouldn't have any trouble driving back home later in the dark.

When she'd been in town with Gino, he'd pointed out various landmarks and items of interest, among them a movie theater.

It was playing an Arnold Schwarzenegger film. Ally had seen a few of them and decided it would be fascinating to watch one in Italian.

After parking the truck along the side of the street like everyone else did, she went inside and bought a ticket.

Distracted by the amount of goodies in the concession stand, she decided to try some Italian chocolate. With her choice made, she walked inside the theater. The film couldn't have been going more than ten minutes.

She found a seat in the middle of the back row where no one was sitting, then sat down to watch the screen.

There was something about the Austrian born actor trying to teach the kids in his classroom that made Ally chuckle. When he spoke in Italian, it was even funnier. She found herself laughing out loud, something she hadn't done in ages.

"*Scusi, signora.*" An attractive guy, beautifully dressed, who looked to be about her age, sat down next to her, bumping her arm.

He'd done it on purpose of course. In fact he could have had his pick of seats in the semifull room, but he'd claimed one next to her.

He said something else to her in Italian.

She said, "*Scusi, signore.* No Italian."

If he didn't move in about one second, she would.

Naturally he refused to budge. "You are from America. *Si*?" What an incredibly bad idea it had been to sit alone.

"You dance with me after?"

Ally started to get up when another man sat down on her other side. She panicked when he put his arm around her shoulders.

"Sorry I'm late," he spoke into her ear.

She jerked her head around, assailed by the familiar scent clinging to his skin.

"Gino—"

She'd never been so happy to see anyone in her life.

"I've missed you, too, *bellissima*," he whispered against her lips before capturing her mouth.

He drew her close like a lover who'd been anticipating this moment and could no longer hold back.

Ally had been so caught off guard, her mouth opened to the urgent pressure of his and she found herself kissing him back in a slow, languorous giving and taking she'd never experienced in her life.

The background laughter of the crowd faded. All Ally was cognizant of was the throbbing of her heart against his solid male chest. The armrest between them might as well have been nonexistent.

Incredulous when she realized the moaning sounds she heard were coming from her own throat, she finally tore her lips from his and sat back in her seat, completely breathless and ashamed she'd gotten so carried away.

"That other man has gone. Thank you for the convincing performance," she blurted when she could find her voice again. "It got me out of a difficult predicament."

"A word of warning," Gino said in a masterful tone. "Don't ever come to a place like this alone. I want your promise."

"You have it."

"Sitting back here by yourself is an open invitation."

"I know. I simply wasn't thinking." She swallowed hard. "How did you know I was here?"

"When I got home, Bianca told me you'd gone out in the truck. So I asked Paolo to drive me around until I spotted it in front of the theater. You're a fan of this film?"

"Yes."

"So am I. Let's enjoy the rest of the film, shall we?"

It was so exciting to be sitting here with him like this, she could only nod.

"How about some of that chocolate? Your mouth tasted so delicious, I've got to have more."

She thought he wanted some of her candy, but he leaned over and started kissing her again.

"No, Gino." She pushed at his shoulder with her free hand. "There's no one around me now."

"I hadn't noticed," he murmured, giving her another thorough kiss before letting her go.

Without asking her permission, he popped a piece of chocolate into his mouth.

Then he clasped her hand possessively, and sat back to enjoy the movie.

She knew what he was doing. No other man in the theater would dare approach her now. She had her own personal bodyguard to protect her.

She never watched the rest of the film. She was much too conscious of the gorgeous man sitting too close to her. He kept caressing her palm with his thumb, filling her body with desire.

Every touch made it impossible to concentrate on anything else.

At the end of the movie, the lights went on.

Gino slid his hand up her back to her neck and walked her out of the theater to the truck. He asked for the keys.

She fumbled in her purse for them. "Here."

After helping her in the passenger side, he went around to the driver's seat and started the engine.

"Do you often conduct business into the evening?"

Once they merged with the traffic, he darted her a piercing glance. "Only if I want to get everything out of the way so I have all of tomorrow off to spend with my family."

Ally bowed her head, relieved he hadn't been with Merlina for any reason.

"Sofia will be delighted."

"What about you? How does another picnic by the river sound? This time we'll take Leonora with us so the girls can get acquainted."

"I think it's an excellent idea. Sofia needs more interaction with girls her own age."

"Agreed. If you'll give her a morning violin lesson, we can leave afterward and enjoy the rest of the day."

His fingers played with the curls near her nape. His touch sent a yielding feeling of delight through her body. She was still trembling from the kisses they'd shared in the theater.

Terrified Gino would think this widow was falling in far too easily with his plans, especially after the kisses they'd just shared she decided to bring up the subject she'd been putting off.

"Gino—I wonder if you would do me a favor."

"Of course."

"I've been waiting for you to give my husband's laptop back to me."

She heard his sharp intake of breath. "If you were hoping to see the pictures, they've been deleted."

She recrossed her legs. "You had no right to do that."

"You didn't want to see them. Trust me."

Ally swallowed hard. "Were they all of Donata?"

"Yes, if that's any consolation."

"It isn't."

A sound broke from his throat. "I swear I didn't look at anything else. While you were in jail, I was so determined you were up to no good, I didn't take the time to look at the e-mails or anything else your husband might have stored in there."

"I believe you." She'd found out for herself that Gino was a man of uncommon integrity.

After a pregnant pause he said, "If you didn't know what was in the laptop, why did you bring it to Europe?"

"It's a long story…" her voice trailed.

"I'd like to hear it. We've got all night."

Since he knew her most painful secret anyway, what did it matter if she satisfied his curiosity.

"On my way out the door of my condo to drive to the airport, I listened to one of my phone messages. It was a man asking to talk to Jim." After she explained everything to Gino she said, "Since I needed to get to the airport, and Troy had just been cleaning out lockers, I couldn't very well ask him to keep the laptop until I returned. So I put it in my suitcase.

"I would have taken a look after I reached St. Moritz, but realized I didn't have an adaptor."

Gino made a strange sound in his throat. "When we get back home, feel free to use my study."

"Thank you," she whispered shakily.

"You might not thank me later if you find anything that could be hurtful."

"I'm past being shocked, Gino."

"Until I saw those photos, I thought I was, too."

CHAPTER SIX

BEFORE long they pulled into the courtyard of the farmhouse and went inside. Without preamble he guided her into his study off the foyer. It was a cozy room with print curtains, leather chairs and couches, books and paintings.

"Sit down at my desk."

While she did his bidding, he opened the closet and pulled the laptop from the shelf.

After placing it in front of her, he opened a drawer and reached for an adaptor, then plugged the cord into the wall.

"I'll leave you to it while I say good night to my family."

His handsome features were marred by lines that made him look older. He left the room, shutting the door behind him.

Haunted by the change in his demeanor, since she'd mentioned the laptop, Ally was almost afraid to open it. Though she'd insisted that nothing could bother her now, it was obvious Gino wasn't convinced. Neither was she…

After a minute she found the courage to turn the computer on. Evidently Jim hadn't bothered with a password or Gino wouldn't have been able to see those photographs.

She booted up the system. Soon the home page Jim had created flashed on the screen.

Ally's eyes darted to the favorite pictures icon. Gino had said he'd deleted them. There was one way to find out, but something held her back and she clicked on the e-mail account.

Ally wasn't at all surprised to discover it full of messages from the same person.

She opened the top one he'd received in January before leaving for Switzerland.

I feel the same way, *amore mia*. Everything is now done.
I'll be waiting for you in our usual place with a car my husband can't trace. Once we reach the port, the family yacht will be waiting for us. We'll sail directly to Sicily where we'll be home free. Did I say that right?
Hurry!

Ally felt as if she'd just been slugged in the stomach.

She scrolled below to an earlier message he'd sent Donata.

That's how I felt the first day we met. Luckily for me Ally isn't the suspicious type. She's too into her music and has no idea I'm leaving her for good. I don't know what she'd do if she ever found out. Probably turn into a bitter woman like her mother.

It'll be much better if I disappear. She'll never know you and I are together. I live to be with you, Donata. You know that don't you? You're the fulfillment of my every fantasy.

The depth of Jim's deception left Ally speechless. Her eyes held a faraway look because she knew it was the real Jim talking.

No doubt Donata had been a true beauty, but more importantly, she'd had the right credentials Ally's husband required.

To think Ally had spent four months sobbing for her loss when Jim had been making plans to run away forever.

Compelled to read on, she opened the e-mail further down.

I've told you my husband changed into a very suspicious and calculating man. He would never allow a divorce. If he knew what I was planning, he would have me committed for insanity because he has that kind of power.

That's why I've asked you to be patient until I've made all the financial arrangements so nothing goes wrong.

Now that you've come into my life, I want only you.

Sickened by what she was reading, Ally buried her face in her hands. Though Jim and Donata might have been full grown adults, they talked like two naughty children who didn't have the emotional capacity to feel anyone else's pain.

Jim's poor parents who lived in Eugene—the knowledge of what their son had done would be so damaging, she didn't know if she could ever bring herself to tell them the truth.

Or her mother—especially not her mother who'd never trusted men since Ally's father had walked out on them when she was two.

Ally mulled over the revelations Jim never thought she'd see.

He'd met his match in Donata. If anyone was calculating, it was Sofia's mother. No wonder Gino was desperate to protect his niece from any more pain.

If Troy hadn't been super conscientious about his job, Ally would be clueless about the extent of their betrayal.

But since these e-mails *did* exist, and Ally was in possession of them, then Gino had every right to read them, too. She was heartsick to think he and Sofia had been forced to wait *four* months to hear any news about Donata.

When he read these and found out what exactly Donata and Jim had been planning, he'd be beyond angry.

So was Ally. Enraged was more like it! Enraged over the injury they'd done to their families on both sides of the Atlantic without counting the cost.

She was appalled at their utter selfishness and cruelty.

It was one thing to have an affair. But to run away together and let their loved ones wonder what had happened? Ally couldn't comprehend it. As far as she was concerned, she and Gino's family were the victims here.

If Jim had told Ally he'd met someone else, she would have suffered, but in the end she would have agreed to a divorce. Could anything be worse than trying to hold on to a man who didn't know the meaning of love?

It had taken Jim with his blond tennis star looks, and his hunger for a woman of Donata's class and money, to charm her into disappearing with him. As long as she brought her inheritance with her, of course.

The whole thing was absurd. Outrageous!

Ally flung herself out of the chair and raced over to the door to find Gino.

She was in such a hurry, she didn't see him until they practically collided in the hallway. He put out his hands to steady her.

She tried not to be affected by his nearness, but it was impossible. The feel of his hands on her arms sent tingles of sensation through her body.

His jet-black eyes assessed her relentlessly. "I knew I shouldn't have left you alone."

"It's horrible in a way I would never have anticipated, Gino." She tiptoed so she could whisper in his ear. "Sofia must never find out."

He relinquished his hold and rushed into the study ahead of her.

She closed the door behind her. "I made the mistake of reading the top e-mail first. If you start at the bottom, it will read in chronological order," she explained unnecessarily.

Since she already knew what was in the e-mails, there was no point in reliving something she wanted wiped from her memory, so she stood in front of the desk and waited.

An electric silence filled the room before Gino exploded with a string of expletives. Suddenly he shot to his feet. One glimpse of the wild fury in his eyes caused her to tremble.

"I knew she was capable of a lot of things," he

muttered in a lethal tone, "but to forget she'd ever given birth—"

Ally rubbed her arms to try to stop the shivering. "I know," she whispered. "There's no mention of Sofia, no mention of your brother's illness. Yet she had Jim believing her husband was a cruel, calculating man."

Gino stared at her through eyes that had become black slits. "She was describing *me*, not Marcello. *I* wasn't the one blind to her faults from the beginning. She hated me for that."

His fingers made furrows through his vibrant black hair. "Ever since I repelled Donata's advances, and refused to give her money, she's been telling stories out of school about me to the tabloids."

Stunned by his words Ally said, "What kind of stories?"

His features looked like chiseled stone. "The one where I was in love with her first, but she preferred my brother. In my jealousy, I would do anything to have her for myself…"

Ally groaned.

"It's true I met her before he did. A mutual friend of our family gave a party. Marcello had the flu and couldn't go, but I did. The host introduced me to Donata who'd come from Rome. She *was* exceptionally beautiful," Gino admitted, "but let's just say she didn't appeal to me. I left the party never expecting to see her again.

"A few months later I found out Marcello had met her at another party. He fell hard for her.

"The last thing I expected was that she would end up my sister-in-law. It was the only time I remember my brother having made a bad choice about something, or someone. Of course I wouldn't have let him know it. I loved him and wished for his happiness above all else."

She folded her arms tightly against her waist. Gino carried an even heavier burden than she'd realized.

"For what it's worth, Gino, if Donata had told my husband the truth about her family situation, Jim wouldn't have cared. He wanted Donata because she was the personification of everything he desired. After we were married I learned that he felt entitled to live a life he hadn't been born to. I'm convinced that's why he worked in Europe, so he could prey on women like your sister-in-law. As you said, she was beautiful," her voice trailed.

"She couldn't hold a candle to you."

"Spare me the platitudes, Gino."

He flashed her a rapier glance. "If you don't think I meant it, take the advice you gave Sofia and look in the mirror. It will remove any doubts."

She shook her head in denial. "This isn't about me."

He moved closer to her. "Did you know your

marriage was in trouble before he was found with Donata?"

She rubbed her temples where she could feel another headache coming on.

Finally she turned to him.

"When my husband didn't get off the plane in Portland four months ago, I hired a detective to look for him.

"It took two months before I was told Jim and another woman were found dead together. It validated my suspicions that he'd been unfaithful for some time."

"How long were you married?"

"Two and a half years, but it was during the latter half that he spent longer times in Switzerland, always phoning with an excuse of some kind for not coming home sooner. Somewhere, deep down, I knew he was lying, but I wouldn't admit it to myself."

She heard a savage sound come out of her host. It made her shiver all over again.

"Donata did the same thing. She'd be gone for long periods, then call and say she'd been detained. It killed Sofia every damn time that happened."

Ally's eyes filled with liquid. "The poor darling. I'm just thankful it's over so she's not still waiting for the phone to ring, or for her mother to walk in the house."

Gino nodded, but he looked so drawn it alarmed Ally.

"Six days ago, the detective who'd worked on my husband's disappearance called me into his office. He told me about Donata. At that point I felt driven to fly to Europe to see if I could get a few more answers. How ironic to think they were hiding in Jim's computer all this time. Now that I've read the e-mails, everything is crystal clear."

She took a deep breath. "I'll leave it up to you to destroy the laptop and everything in it. Now if you'll excuse me, I'm tired and want to go to bed."

She left the room and hurried upstairs, more wounded for Sofia than anything else. Donata had planned to abandon her own daughter! Ally was so deeply hurt for that precious girl, Jim's rejection of Ally hardly made a dent.

She tried to imagine Gino going off with some woman never to be seen again, but she couldn't because he was a different breed of human being. Decent, honorable. Willing to give his all for everyone's happiness without having anyone to support him.

Marcello had been Gino's best friend. To be denied it now because of his illness while trying to be both mother and father to Sofia would place an enormous strain on Gino. Ally was glad that for a little while she could be here to ease his burden in some small way.

Before washing her face, she happened to glance in the mirror. There was a speck of chocolate on her cheek, but it appeared Gino had kissed away her lipstick. Despite the new revelations in the e-mails, just remembering the sensation of his male mouth devouring hers left her breathless and pushed everything else to the back of her mind, even after she'd turned out the light and had climbed under the covers.

Her heart did a little kick when she realized he was taking all of them to the river again tomorrow. She found herself counting the hours.

After a few minutes she turned on her side and reached for the vase of lavender, needing to breathe in its fragrance one more time. She'd never been given flowers for no reason before.

When Gino had handed them to her with that glint in his black eyes, she felt like she'd just been handed the world.

It was after two in the morning when Gino shut off the computer and went up to bed. He'd read through dozens of back pages of e-mails. There were dozens more but he didn't have the stomach for it.

He couldn't get his mind off Ally who didn't seem to know how truly wonderful she was. It explained her vulnerability, put there by a man who hadn't known how to love anyone but himself.

Unfortunately even if the fire had gone out of her marriage, Gino knew love wasn't always that cut and dried. Marcello had said as much when he'd admitted that he and Donata weren't going to make it. "I wish I were a faucet, Gino, so I could turn off certain feelings."

In Marcello's case the illness had done it for him.

Where Ally was concerned, Gino feared that deep down in her psyche, she still had some feelings for her husband in spite of what he'd done to her.

Gino couldn't fathom the other man not cherishing her, not wanting to come home to their bed every night.

He paused on the second floor, fighting the overwhelming impulse to knock on her door and ask if he could come in. He wanted to tell her how beautiful she was—show her.

Before Marcello's illness, when Gino had been playing the field with no intention of settling down, Marcello had warned him that one day there'd be a woman who would bring him to his knees. Gino had laughed at his brother, but he wasn't laughing now.

His limbs felt heavy as he climbed to the third floor. Tonight he would pray for sleep to come quickly.

When his phone roused him from oblivion at

six in the morning, he realized he'd gotten his wish and cursed the person who dared to call him this early. On a groan, he reached for his cell.

It was Carlo. That brought him awake in a hurry.

"What's going on, Carlo?"

"I'm afraid you could be in trouble, Gino. I've arranged for us to meet in Rome with Alberto Toscano at nine this morning. That gives you three hours to arrange your affairs."

Gino levered himself off the bed. Toscano was one of Italy's top criminal defense attorneys.

"Don't tell me that insane story about the tampered brakes has grown legs—"

"I've just seen the forensics report on the car. There was definitely foul play involved."

Gino's eyes closed tightly as his mind grappled with the stunning news.

"It gets worse, Gino. The prosecutor has discovered that Signora Parker was in St. Moritz. He's trying to link the dots that prove she collaborated with you to carry out this crime."

A groan came out of Gino.

"I'll fill you in later. *Ciao.*"

The line went dead.

In the middle of the violin lesson, Bianca came in the living room. "Forgive me for interrupting but Leonora's papa just dropped her off and Gino's not here to make the introductions."

"No problem, Bianca. Bring her in here."

Ally sensed Sofia's disappointment, but it really was better for her to start making new friends.

"Hello," Ally said as the housekeeper ushered Leonora in the room. "I'm Ally, and this is Sofia. We're so glad you've come over."

"Thank you. I wanted to come before, but Mama said my fever had to go away first."

"Do you feel better now?" Sofia asked.

"Yes." The girl was shorter than Sofia with dark blond hair. "You're so lucky to be learning the violin."

"I think so, too. Do you want to hear Ally play?"

"I'd love it!"

The girl was so warm and natural, Ally was charmed by her.

"All right. One small piece. How about something from Peter and the Wolf?"

"What's that?" both girls asked at the same time.

"You haven't heard of it before?"

They shook their heads.

"Well, it tells a story, and each instrument represents one of the characters. The music you're going to hear is Peter's theme song."

Ally had always loved it. When she finished playing, Leonora acted as enraptured as Sofia.

"I wish I could play."

Ally looked at Sofia. "Why don't I give my violin to Leonora, and you can show her what you've learned."

Leonora's dark eyes sparkled. "You would let me?"

"Of course. Have fun you two."

Ally ducked out of the living room, delighted to realize the violins were a perfect ice breaker.

With time on her hands waiting for Gino, she walked to the kitchen to get a piece of fruit from the bowl on the table.

Bianca met her at the doorway. "I didn't want to say anything in front of Sofia, but Gino had to go to Rome on unexpected business for his brother this morning. He's not sure when he'll be back."

Ally's spirits plummeted, but she didn't dare let the housekeeper know how the news had affected her.

"That's fine. If Paolo is willing, I'll take the girls to the river as planned and have another picnic."

Bianca looked relieved. "That's good for Sofia. I'll get everything ready."

"Let me help. I don't have anything else to do."

"*Bene.*"

They worked in harmony while sounds of a violin lesson being given drifted through the house to the kitchen.

Bianca smiled. "Sofia is very happy since you came."

"She's a lovely girl."

"Gino is happier, too. Everyone is glad you are going to stay."

Only until July, Bianca...

Ten minutes later Sofia and Leonora came running into the kitchen.

"Ally? Have you seen Rudolfo? Leonora wants to watch my cat do tricks."

"Have you checked the terrace? He likes to sun himself on the swing this time of day."

"That's right! Come on, Leonora."

They dashed out again.

The two women exchanged an amused glance.

"I'm going upstairs to change into my swimming suit."

"While you do that, I'll call Paolo and have him bring the car around."

"Thank you for making me feel so welcome, Bianca."

"It's my pleasure, *signora*."

As she left the kitchen, she turned to Bianca. "Please call me Ally." Bianca nodded and waved her off.

The trip to the river turned out to be an all day affair. Toward evening Ally asked Paolo to drive them into Remo where they enjoyed a pasta dinner al fresco before driving Leonora home.

By the time they returned to the farmhouse, Sofia looked pleasantly tired. They'd all picked up some sun.

Sofia gave Ally a hug. "Thank you for a wonderful day. Now I'd better go see how Papa is doing."

"I'm sure he's missed you."

Despite the fact that Gino hadn't been able to join them, it *had* been a wonderful day.

After reaching for the picnic basket, she started for the kitchen door. That's when she heard the sounds of a car coming into the courtyard. When she looked around she saw an unfamiliar sports car pull into the detached garage. It was Gino!

He looked impossibly attractive in a light gray suit and tie. Her heart skipped a dozen beats.

He walked toward her with his gaze narrowed on her face.

"I'm sorry about today, Ally. It couldn't be helped."

"You don't have to explain to me. It's fine."

"I called the house just now. Bianca said Sofia and Leonora had a fabulous time with you at the river."

"We did."

"Even before the violin lessons started, my niece felt a bond with you. After today her attachment to you is much stronger."

"Then it's good I'm leaving at the end of the

month. I can't let her become too emotionally dependent on me."

"She already is." His voice sounded like it had come from a deep, underground cavern.

"I wish you hadn't said that. It worries me how vulnerable she is right now."

"I'm glad you recognize it because the end of June will be here before we know it. She'll be crushed if you talk about leaving."

Ally sucked in her breath. "But that was our arrangement, Gino. If I were to stay longer, it will only hurt her more when I have to go."

"That was Donata's pattern. Come and go at will, regardless of Sofia's pain."

Heat swamped her cheeks. "How dare you compare me to Donata! I'm not Sofia's mother, but if I were," her voice trembled, "I'd love that child and do everything in my power to help her feel safe and happy for the rest of her life!"

He took a step closer. "I believe you really mean that."

"Of course I do. I already love her," Ally admitted before she realized she'd said too much. "Who wouldn't?" she cried out to cover her mistake.

"Her own mother, for one," Gino responded with bitter irony. "Her own father for another, although through no fault of his own. That leaves me, her uncle, who might not be able to protect her much longer."

Ally stared at him mystified. "Bianca said you had to leave on some urgent business for Marcello."

"I lied."

Her hands curled into fists. "If you're trying to scare me, you're doing a good job of it." He still didn't say anything.

"Gino—" she exploded. "I'm starting to get really frightened."

"That makes two of us. Give me an hour to shower and say good night to my family, then meet me on the terrace. We have to talk."

In a few swift strides he was gone.

CHAPTER SEVEN

TREMBLING with anxiety, Ally followed at a slower pace. After putting the basket on the kitchen counter, she went upstairs to shower, too. A day in the hot sun had made her messy and sticky. But Gino had upset her so much, she went through the motions of washing her hair and getting dressed without conscious thought.

He said he needed an hour. She gave him another fifteen minutes before going down to the living room.

The French doors to the terrace were ajar. With her heart pounding so hard she felt slightly sick, she stepped outside. The first thing she saw beyond the patio furniture was Gino's tall, masculine silhouette standing there in the darkness. The only light came from a slip of a moon that had just appeared above the horizon. Once again she was reminded of the way he'd looked to her the night he'd taken her to jail—like the fierce, proud falcon of his namesake.

He made an intimidating presence standing there with his legs slightly apart, his arms folded. He eyed her with frightening solemnity. She put a nervous hand to her throat.

"It's obvious something terrible has happened. Tell me what it is."

His mouth had become a tight thin line.

"So far Sofia knows her mother died in a car accident. Period. That's all I want her to know."

"I realize that. Let's hope and pray she never learns the true circumstances. At least not until she's a lot older."

"That's the idea," he bit out, "but something's come up beyond my ability to control, let alone stop."

The blood in Ally's veins started to chill. "What is it?"

"A few days ago the first stories about the accident came out in the paper with the usual sensational lies attached. This time they took the tack that foul play was involved."

She frowned. "Foul play? It was an accident! One of the Swiss authorities drove me to the bridge and explained what happened. He told me the blow to both their skulls had been caused by the bridge's beams when the car plunged into the river."

"Ally—" he said in a tortured whisper. "This is going to be hard for you to hear. The forensics report on the car came back a few days ago. It proved that the brakes had been tampered with."

She reeled. *"What?"*

"I'm afraid it means someone wanted your husband and Donata out of the way permanently."

She shook her head in disbelief. "Who?"

He drew in a deep breath. "In the words of the police, a jealous husband or wife who caught the two of them together and committed a crime of passion at the height of their pain."

"But that's preposterous! Marcello is incapacitated, and I was home in Portland when the accident happened."

"That's true," he muttered.

It took a minute for his words to sink in. When they did, her head flew back.

"They're not trying to say *you* did it?"

His face became an inscrutable mask. "Based on past lies generated by Donata herself, the prosecutor is convinced I'm guilty. He's already building his argument to present to the judge. It's a process not unlike your grand juries in the States. If the judge feels the prosecutor has a strong case, it'll go to trial. If I'm convicted by a jury, I could go to prison for life."

She couldn't credit what he'd just told her.

"On what evidence?"

"For one thing, I went on several overnight searches in January looking for Donata. I can't prove that I wasn't in Switzerland at the time the accident occurred."

"But that's not proof of anything!"

This couldn't be happening…

As her thoughts darted ahead to the possibility that he might be arrested, she clung to the side of the patio swing for support.

"If that happened, who could possibly take care of your family? It would kill Sofia!"

Silence followed her outburst. Her gaze flew to his once more.

He stared at her for a long moment.

"If anything happens to me, I only know one person beyond all else I could trust to do the right thing for both of them."

"W-who is it?" She didn't think it could be a distant relative or he would have mentioned it sooner.

"A woman I'm planning to marry in a few days."

Marry?

Ally wasn't able to hide the gasp that escaped her throat.

If she'd been shot, the pain inflicted couldn't possibly have hurt her the way this shocking piece of news did. She still hadn't recovered from being in his arms when he'd kissed her senseless in the movie theater.

For a moment she'd thought—

Oh, what a fool she'd been to think they'd

meant anything to him beyond getting rid of the other man who'd been annoying her.

"I see." She struggled to keep her voice steady. "Does she know you're suspected of a crime that could put you in prison?"

"Yes."

Suddenly Ally had difficulty forming words. She swallowed a low moan.

"Does Sofia know her?"

"Yes."

It had to be one of his girlfriends. "Does Sofia like her?"

"Yes."

Ally refused to face him. "Then why haven't you married her before now?"

Her question rang in the night air. She hoped no one in the house heard her.

"The time wasn't right."

"But now it is? Just at the moment when you could be arrested and taken away?"

"Yes. There's no other way."

She forgot her promise not to look at him and swung around in his direction.

"Don't you think that's unfair to this woman?"

"Totally."

"Stop being so glib, Gino. I'm trying to have a conversation with you."

One of his black brows lifted. "I thought we were having one."

Red stained her skin. "You know what I meant. But all you do is answer in monosyllables."

Again there was no response.

"Does Sofia know what you're planning?"

"Not yet. I thought we'd tell her together in the morning."

"You mean the woman you're going to marry will be here so the two of you can talk it over with Sofia?"

"Yes. I hope that puts your mind at ease. Now you won't have to worry about my niece clinging to you."

"I was worried about it for *her* sake, not mine," she defended quietly, hurt to the quick by his comment.

"I'm well aware of that fact, Ally. So let's agree you'll go on giving her lessons until the wedding."

"But if that's only in a few days, then I'll leave at the same time, and—"

"No. You won't be going anywhere. I'm planning to take Sofia on our short honeymoon. After we get back, she'll resume her lessons."

The mention of a honeymoon tore Ally up inside.

"I—I'm sure Sofia will love being with both of you, but when you return, your wife won't want another woman in the house. I'm sure if you talk to the owner at the music store in Remo, he'll supply you with names of several violin instructors who would love to teach your niece."

He shifted his weight. "I'm afraid it's too soon to be switching teachers on her. You've become her heroine. No one else will do."

Afraid to hear anymore she said, "If that's all, then I'll say good night."

"Not yet," he muttered. "There's something important we still haven't touched on."

"What?" She needed to be alone where she could give in to this fresh new pain.

"The matter of an attorney for you."

The shocks just kept coming. "I don't understand."

"My friend Carlo informed me the prosecutor hasn't ruled you out as a coconspirator."

She blinked. "On what grounds?"

"That you conspired with me to get revenge on your husband and Donata. Maybe you didn't do the actual deed, but you'd be held equally to blame under the law. The insurance policy your husband took out on you before he left for Switzerland in January could have provided an additional motive for you to join forces with me."

She shook her head in utter bewilderment. "How did he know about the insurance?"

"Yesterday the prosecutor's office talked to the detective in Oregon who's been working with you on your husband's disappearance. The case against you isn't nearly as strong, but I'm afraid you're going to need legal counsel, too."

Ally had gone numb inside. "When I get home, I'll retain one."

"How will you do that on your salary? You won't be able to afford the kind you need."

She lifted anguished eyes to his. "What else haven't you told me about the case?"

She heard him draw in a deep breath. "My attorney, Signore Toscano, said that your appearance in Switzerland the other day would lead the prosecutor to think you'd flown over to visit the scene of the crime you and I planned. It's not unusual for a criminal to do that.

"He suggested that since you're already here in Italy, and haven't yet contacted a criminal lawyer, he believes it will be to our advantage if he represents both of us."

"But, Gino— That's impossible! Besides the fact that I could never afford him, it would be a conflict of interest. In order for him to represent both of us, I'd have to be your wife."

"Exactly."

"But you're getting married soon."

"That's right. If you'd asked me, I would have told you the name of my bride-to-be. She's an American named Allyson Cummings Parker from Portland, Oregon."

The shock of his words propelled her into the swing. She sat down with such force, it rocked back and forth.

He came to stand in front of her and stopped the motion with his hand. When their legs brushed against each other, he made no move to allow her breathing room.

"I know your heart, Ally. When you discovered what your husband had done, you felt compassion for Marcello and didn't hesitate to fly here to talk to him.

"Even at the height of your own pain, even at the risk of getting into trouble by defying me, you put Marcello's welfare ahead of your own.

"I've never known a man or woman with your kind of selflessness and courage.

"No matter how I treated you in the jail, you wouldn't break down because you didn't want to repeat anything to the wrong ears. I owe you everything for your discretion."

"No, Gino. Any woman in my position would have done the same thing."

His eyes glimmered with a strange light. "No. You're one in a million. Now I have a way to repay you.

"If we're married, then we can't be forced to testify against each other. My money will ensure the toughest defense attorney there is. Best of all, if anything happens to me, you'll be there to raise Sofia and watch over Marcello.

"Once you take my name, you'll inherit all that I possess, and you'll be given power of attorney to run my brother's affairs until Sofia turns eighteen and takes over her birthright."

He leaned closer, bringing his face within inches of hers.

"Before you come up with a dozen reasons why you can't marry me, tell me exactly what there is for you to go home to. Certainly not a husband who was unworthy of you.

"If it's a matter of leaving the orchestra, we have excellent orchestras here. Any conductor hearing you would hire you on the spot.

"Sofia told me about your mother. If you'd like her and your aunt with you, we have a whole palazzo for them to stay in.

"Sofia also told me you wanted a family, but your husband died before that could happen. I've seen the way you interact with my niece. She'll fill your heart the way she fills mine.

"If you and I have to stand trial, I'll testify that you had nothing to do with the accident, which will only be the truth. If I have to go to prison, and it's still a big if at this point, it will help me to survive knowing my brother and niece will be in your care. You'll be a wealthy woman who can do with the money as you see fit.

"Should the real culprit be apprehended and brought to justice, then we'll reassess our situation and go from there.

"Don't dismiss this out of hand, Ally. I love my

family more than my own life." His voice shook. "You're the one person I trust to watch over them and see to their needs like you would your own family. There's a goodness and purity in your character that sets you apart from the other women I've known. Sofia could never go wrong under your guidance.

"As for Marcello, your gentleness to him the second you realized his condition was a revelation. Both Bianca and Marcello's nurses have remarked on it.

"They like you very much already. All the staff will be faithful to you should I have to go away.

"Think about it tonight, Ally, and we'll talk in the morning before breakfast."

He brushed her lips with his own, then left the terrace.

Ally sat stationary in the swing, unable to make a sound. She'd never heard anyone pour out their soul to her the way he'd just done.

Though Gino needed her to say yes to his marriage proposal, what he was really asking was that she enter into a sacred trust with him.

He wasn't offering his love. How could he? He hadn't known her long enough for that miracle to happen—if it could at all.

But should the unspeakable occur and he had to go to prison, she could understand how desperate he was to get his affairs in order first.

In return for becoming his wife, she would be getting something entirely different: financial security, his name and protection, a home and the chance to be a mother to a girl who needed one, the opportunity to be a caregiver to a cherished brother.

Should she marry him and he was arrested, she would have the kind of money Jim once dreamed about.

With it she could hire the manpower necessary to find the real killer and free Gino.

She sat there for a long time deep in thought.

It was well after midnight when she finally left the terrace and went up to her room.

After preparing for bed, she got under the covers, tossing and turning as her thoughts drifted back to Jim and the way they'd met.

When she'd literally run into him while they were both skiing at Mount Hood, there'd been an attraction that had led to serious dating and marriage. But after the first few months following their honeymoon, the passion didn't seem as intense. He started doing more ski shows in other parts of the country like Tahoe and Vail. The shows coincided with her concerts so they were spending more time apart. But it was the show in Las Vegas that brought about a major change in their marriage.

Jim met a Swiss promoter who offered to let him sell Slippery Slopes skiwear in St. Moritz on a trial basis. It meant being out of the country for big blocks of time.

Of course Ally had wanted him to be successful so he could realize his dream to be the owner of the company one day. But as she'd learned on her honeymoon, he'd had bigger dreams than that. Ones in which her input didn't matter to him. She'd only been a stepping stone on his way to bigger and better things.

How different in every way it was from her experience with Gino who knew his place in life and was steady as the sun coming up every morning. A man who put everyone's comfort ahead of his own and found joy being with the family he loved.

There was nothing shallow or selfish about him. Dear God how she loved him!

No one at home, not her family or friends would understand if she married Gino only four months after burying her husband.

What they didn't realize was that she'd been out of love with Jim longer than she'd been in love. But it had taken a remarkable man like Gino to remove the blinkers so she could see how empty her life had been with Jim, how barren.

Just being with Gino filled all those desolate places inside her. He was like a hot fire she rushed to embrace after coming in out of the freezing cold.

She knew that neither she nor any woman

would have been his choice if the circumstances had been different.

The fact that he wasn't married yet proved it. But the precarious situation in which he found himself forced him to reach out to her because he knew he could trust her.

After her experience with Jim, she realized trust was the key element in a solid marriage if it was going to work…trust and the incredible passion she already felt for Gino.

Only time would tell if he could ever come to love her, let alone with that same intensity. But how could she compete when there'd been real beauties in his life like Merlina?

Still—Gino had turned to Ally in his darkest hour. Though he hadn't mentioned them having a child of their own, it was something she wanted with every fiber of her being. If he wanted a child, too, that would be a sign that he expected to sleep with her and make her his wife in every way.

Just thinking about lying in his arms made her breathless. She wanted to give him his answer now, but it was only four in the morning.

He expected to talk to her before breakfast. Since Bianca served it at seven-thirty, that wasn't too far off. She set her watch alarm for seven before catching a few hours sleep.

When she heard the little tinkle of the bell three

hours later, she slid out of bed to shower. Normally she would be exhausted, but with Gino waiting for her, her adrenaline was working overtime.

Once dressed, with her curls brushed and fresh makeup, she hurried downstairs. The housekeeper was already up and busy in the kitchen.

"Good morning, Bianca. Have you seen Gino yet?"

"*Si*. He's outside changing a tire on the truck."

"Thank you."

Ally left the kitchen through the side door to find him. Her heart was skipping all over the place.

A flash of pink caught Gino's attention. The sight of Ally moving toward him in a T-shirt and jeans her body filled out to perfection caused him to pause in his task of tightening the lug nuts.

If he didn't miss his guess, she hadn't been able to sleep, either. She walked with purpose, a sign that he feared didn't bode well for the desired outcome. But he was prepared for any hurdle she was determined to put in his way.

"*Buon giorno*, Ally."

"Good morning. I didn't realize we'd driven home on a flat tire the other night."

"It felt low, so I decided to change it, just to be on the safe side."

He put the wrench back in his toolbox, then dusted off his hands.

The sun had just come up over the lavender fields. Standing there in the early morning rays that gilded her hair and brought out the startling green of her eyes staring through to his soul, she looked like a piece of chocolate he would give anything to devour. But it wasn't the right time or place. Not yet…

If she was hoping he would help her find an opening, then she would have a long wait.

"After learning that someone caused that accident, I'm afraid I got very little sleep last night. I don't care how much circumstantial evidence the prosecutor says he has, I can't believe the case against either of us will go to trial. But on the outside chance that I'm wrong, I—I'll marry you provided we stay married until Sofia's eighteen."

Gino fought not to reveal his elation. He'd feared she would turn him down flat for several reasons he could think of, like the fact that she wasn't in love with him.

As for her ultimatum, there were ways around it. He'd worry about that later. All that mattered right now was her capitulation. "If some monstrous miscarriage of justice puts you in prison, Sofia will need constancy from at least one parent."

"Agreed," he murmured, still holding his breath.

"However if the person who caused that accident is caught, it would be criminal for us to suddenly dissolve the marriage, and for me to go back to the States. Sofia would grieve all over again for another loss."

Gino could scarcely control his joy. "I couldn't have said it better myself."

By the way her chest rose and fell, she still had more to say. He waited eagerly for the rest.

"To this point in time you've avoided marriage."

"I wouldn't have if the right woman had come along. I've been waiting…"

"Yes, well I thought the right man *had* come along, but it turned out I was wrong. After the fiasco of my first marriage, I'm nervous about entering into another one."

"Then we'll both be nervous together."

"Don't tease about this, Gino. This is much too serious for that."

He took a step closer. What he wanted to do was crush her in his arms, but at this early stage it might frighten her off.

"I didn't know I was doing that. I'm only trying to say that since I've never been a husband before, I want to do it right."

"So do I," she whispered. "I want your happiness more than anything."

"You think I don't want the same for you?" he challenged.

"What you've offered me has already made me very happy," her voice throbbed. "I always wanted a family of my own. My father left when I was two. I grew up in a home without him, or siblings or cousins.

"It was hard because my mother was too immersed in her own pain to realize how lonely I felt. Don't get me wrong. She's a wonderful person in every way, but she had a warped vision of men that was hard for me to throw off. My grandparents were the bright spot in my life, but they died early.

"Mom warned me not to marry Jim. She said he was too good-looking just like my father, that he'd never stay faithful.

"I refused to listen to her. I thought—well, it doesn't matter what I thought. The truth is, I married a selfish man, so my dream of a happy home with babies didn't come to fruition.

"I'm almost twenty-nine, Gino. When I found out he'd died, I felt like I was beyond that part of life where anything and everything is possible. Mother kept saying, 'You have your music, honey. It's enough.'

"But when I met Sofia, I knew it *wasn't* enough. I saw myself in her. Because of you, I can have that family I always wanted. Sofia is a joy."

"She is that," he concurred. "As long as we're sharing let me say that any hope I had of finding the right woman and settling down pretty much died when Marcello married Donata and I saw the grief she brought to his life. Her amoral behavior was a huge turnoff. Once Marcello was afflicted with Alzheimer's, I gave up the idea of asking someone to be my wife and take on my niece and her father. It wouldn't be fair to a woman with expectations of starting out the marriage with no responsibilities except to each other.

"As you and I have discovered to our horror, your husband and Donata tried to hide their liaison from everyone, but they came to a surprise ending that caused their secrets to become public knowledge. For that reason, I have no intention of marrying anyone unless it's you. Sofia needs to believe in me, in *us*, Ally. She needs to know that what we have is real and worth imitating when she's old enough to be married. Her parents were never friends. That's what she'll see with us. Therefore there'll be no divorce when she turns eighteen. That's *my* condition."

She lowered her head, not saying anything.

"Ally?" he prodded. "Did you even have friendship with Jim?"

It took a long time before she said, "No."

He could always count on her honesty.

"Then we have more going for us than either of

us has had up to now because my relationships with women to this point haven't had the depth needed to survive over a lifetime."

Slowly she raised her head. "What reason will we give Sofia why we're sleeping in separate bedrooms?"

He'd wondered how long it would take her to get around to that question. There was a nerve throbbing frantically in her throat. It intrigued him no end. Obviously she wasn't quite ready for the big step of going to bed with him yet. He'd give her a little more time to get used to the idea.

"We won't have to tell her anything. By day we'll interact like a happily married couple. At night there's an anteroom off my bedroom. What goes on behind closed doors is our business, no one else's."

There were all kinds of side roads leading home. If necessary Gino would travel down every one of them to reach it.

"Gino?" she whispered tentatively.

"What is it?"

"I'm afraid."

"That makes two of us. But having seen the courageous Ally Parker in action, I'm willing to leap into the fire with you."

He could see her swallowing hard. "I—I'm terrified you might really have to go to prison for something you didn't do."

Deeply moved by her concern he said, "If I have my way, neither of us will be found guilty. In the meantime we have the power to make one special girl happy."

Her green eyes glistened. "If you're sure…"

His chest tightened. "I suppose everything in life is a gamble, but this time I like the odds. Shall we go inside and tell Sofia?"

She bit her lip, drawing his attention to the succulent mouth he'd wanted to taste over and over again the other night. Once he'd coaxed her lips apart, some divine chemistry had been responsible for the rest. Her passionate response had almost caused him to lose control. In a movie theater no less. It had to be a first for him.

Right now it looked like she needed a little help in the confidence department.

He reached for her left hand which was trembling. He stared pointedly at her bare ring finger.

"Where's the wedding ring you once wore?"

"Buried with my husband."

Her stunning answer pleased him in ways he didn't have the time to examine right now.

He felt in his pocket for a certain item. If she didn't fight him on this, then there'd be no going back.

"My mother gave me this before she died. It was her engagement ring. It's unpretentious, just the way she was. The way *you* are.

"She knew I loved nature and encouraged me to be a farmer if that was my choice."

One thing he did know beyond everything else. Ally Parker didn't have an avaricious bone in her gorgeous body, either.

He trapped her gaze with his. "I need you to be very sure before I slide it home on your finger. Is there anything else you want to ask me?"

She moistened her lips nervously. "I can think of a thousand things."

"But?" he prodded.

"But every time I think of what would happen to your family if you were arrested, I get so sick, I *can't* think."

"Then you agree to become a farmer's wife under the worst of circumstances? I can't promise the 'for better' part yet."

A little smile came and went as he slid the gold circle home on her finger. It happened so fast he almost missed it before she looked into his eyes with a haunted expression.

"Surely you once had dreams."

He nodded. "You've made them come true by filling this old farmhouse with heavenly music. The kind the Montefalco family has always loved. Every husband should be so lucky."

As they walked in the house, Gino had no idea Ally's heart was breaking. She'd been waiting to hear him say he wanted to fill his house with children. *Their* children.

But those words hadn't left his lips.

To her chagrin their entrance in the kitchen coincided with the rest of the family's arrival, forcing her to put on a pleasant face when she was dying inside.

While Luigi helped Marcello, Sofia ran around to hug Ally, then Gino.

He swept her up in his arms with an exultant laugh.

Sofia's intelligent eyes studied him. "You look different this morning, Uncle Gino."

"That's because I feel different."

"Why?"

"I'm happy, sweetheart."

Ally's heart plummeted to see what a brilliant performance he was putting on in front of his niece. By now everyone had settled at the table. Gino took his place across from Ally. Once Bianca served them, Gino said, "I have an announcement to make."

Ally felt close to fainting. "Is it that surprise you told me about a few days ago?" Sofia asked.

"As a matter of fact it is. I'm taking the family on a trip."

Her eyes brightened. "Where?"

"To the island of Ischia."

"I've never been there."

"You'll love it."

"How soon are we going to go?"

"On Monday."

"Why not today?"

"Because I need the next few days to get ready."

Sofia eyed Ally who was already squirming in her chair, then she looked at her uncle again. "What about my violin lessons?"

"After we get back, you can resume them."

Sofia sent Ally another troubled glance. "What will you do while we're gone?"

"Why don't you ask Ally to come with us," Gino suggested suavely.

"Would you come with us, Ally? Please say yes," she begged.

Ally wasn't immune to the pleading in her voice.

"I'd love to."

In the next instant Sofia's face lit up like a roomful of sunshine. "Have you ever been to Ischia?"

"No, but just the idea that it's an island intrigues me."

"Me, too."

"I have something else very important to tell all of you," Gino broke in. "This includes Luigi, Roberto, Bianca and Paolo."

He shot Ally a piercing black glance that defied her to say or do anything to upset Sofia now.

"On second thought," he added in a silky tone, "maybe I should let Ally be the one to explain since she's equally involved in this decision."

"What is it, Ally?" Sofia asked softly.

Ally's heart palpitated wildly because she realized he'd just thrown her in at the deep end. She had no choice but to swim.

"Y-your uncle Gino has asked me to marry him," she stammered. "How do you feel about that?"

Ally didn't have to wait long to find out. His niece bolted from her chair and came around to hug Ally's neck.

"Last night I told Papa that I hoped Uncle Gino would marry you. Papa always said Uncle Gino was waiting for the perfect woman to come along."

Gino nodded. "My brother always understood me better than anyone else."

Ally avoided looking at Gino right then. "You actually told your father that?"

"I swear it." Sofia crossed herself. "You told Uncle Gino yes, didn't you?"

Ally was in over her head now. She held out her hand for Sofia to see the gold band.

"Grandma's ring!"

"Yes," Ally whispered, but everyone in the room heard her.

Bianca clapped her hands and offered her sincere congratulations. Luigi made a little speech welcoming her to the family. If the staff was surprised by the announcement, they hid it beautifully.

"We're going to be married on Sunday at the church in Remo by Father Angelini," Gino informed them. "After the service we'll drive to Ischia and stay until we feel like coming home again."

Unless the police summoned Gino to Rome, Ally's heart cried.

Sofia kept her arm around Ally's shoulders. "Is your mama going to come for the wedding?"

"She would like to," Ally lied, "but my aunt can't travel that far with her new hip. I'm sure they'll fly over later in the year when she's better."

No way could Ally tell her mother about this yet. That would have to come later. Much later…

If or when her mother did come, she would find Ally in a vastly different situation from the one she'd been in with Jim.

"My mama won't be able to come, either, but *I'll* be there," Sofia assured Ally.

"That's all I could ask for, darling. How would you like to be my bridesmaid?"

"That's an excellent idea." Gino's black eyes gleamed. "Maybe Anna and Leonora would like to be bridesmaids, too. Ally will take you shopping for dresses when she picks out her wedding dress."

Suddenly Sofia pushed herself away from the table. "Excuse me for a minute. I have to call Anna and tell her what's happened!"

After she disappeared from the kitchen, Gino reached across the table to cover Ally's hand. He squeezed her ring finger especially hard.

"You've just seen a miracle before your very eyes. Asking her to be a bridesmaid was inspirational, but then you have all the right instincts."

Ally hoped that was true because she'd just agreed to take on a lifetime responsibility and didn't want to fail.

"I hear someone out in the courtyard," Gino said before removing his hand. "It must be Dizo. I asked him to bring Leonora over again today. Come with me, Ally. I want him to meet my future wife."

Just hearing Gino say it sent a shiver of delight through her body.

She followed him out the door to the driveway where she saw Leonora and her father get out of a truck.

The two men greeted each other warmly. Then Gino turned to Ally and put his arm around her shoulders. The gesture seemed to come so naturally to him, she could hardly credit it. "Ally? This is my friend and manager, Dizo Rossini. You've already met Leonora."

"How do you, *signore*." Ally shook his hand.

His daughter hung on to Gino's arm. "Is she your new girlfriend, Gino?"

"No." He ruffled her dark blond hair. "Ally Parker is my fiancée. We're getting married on Sunday."

The other man whooped in surprise. "You are a sly fox, Gino. Where have you been keeping this beautiful woman all this time?"

"Why don't you tell him, *bellissima*," Gino said to Ally before giving her a quick kiss on the mouth.

Gino didn't play fair, so she'd better get used to it.

"He kidnapped me off a train headed for Rome. I'm afraid one thing led to another," she said poker-faced.

"Ah, Gino. Love has hit you at last. I can see it in your eyes when you look at her."

Dizo winked at her. "He has had many women chase after him. All kinds," he chatted like the old friend he was. "Finally he found a woman *he* had to chase. That is very good."

Gino grinned. "She didn't make it easy for me."

The other man threw back his dark head and laughed. After he sobered, he waved an index finger in front of Gino. "It makes me glad this crazy business about Donata hasn't stopped you from living your life. It's your turn to have all those bambinos you've wanted to help you run the farm. To think they might all be musicians!" He nudged Gino's arm.

Ally kept the smile pasted on her face.

She turned to Leonora. "You can go in the house if you want. Sofia should be off the phone by now."

"Okay."

As she headed for the house, Sofia ran outside with a joyous smile. The difference in that face from the one Ally had seen for the first time a few nights ago almost made Gino's niece unrecognizable.

Ally was doing the right thing for Sofia. But nothing could take away the pain in her heart that Gino wasn't in love with her. It had been too much to ask, and now it was too late to change things. All Ally had to do was look into Sofia's eyes to realize there could be no going back.

Ally followed them in the house so the two men could be alone.

Sofia was full of excitement about the coming wedding and asked Leonora if she wanted to be a bridesmaid, too. While the three of them were in deep conversation in the living room, Gino entered. His dark eyes sent Ally a private message that he wanted to speak to her alone.

"Excuse me, girls. I'll be back later."

"Okay," Sofia said, but her whole attention was focused on what kind of dresses they would wear.

Gino guided Ally into the study and shut the door. She could hear his mind working.

"Tomorrow we have to meet in my attorney's office. It will take a good part of the day, so we're going to have to get a lot accomplished today."

Before he could say anything else there was a knock on the study door.

"That'll be Father Angelini," Gino explained.

"Yesterday I phoned and asked him to drop by. Now that you've agreed to marry me, he needs to talk to us about the ceremony.

"After he leaves, we'll drive into Remo for the marriage license. Once that's done, we can concentrate on shopping and our preparations for the trip to Ischia."

Ally could hardly keep up with him. One minute she was a widow. The next minute she was engaged to be married to this dynamic man who could move mountains with a snap of his fingers.

The way he was acting, there was no murder case pending that could rip her newfound happiness to shreds. Little did Gino know that his mention of an anteroom where one of them could sleep after they were married had plunged her into despair of a whole new kind. But she would hide it from him if it killed her.

CHAPTER EIGHT

"WE'RE almost through, Signora Parker. This is the last document. Sign beneath Gino's signature, please."

Ally eyed Mr. Toscano. "What does this one say?"

During the lengthy process, he'd patiently translated everything from Italian to English for her.

This morning she'd thought Gino had brought her to his attorney's office to talk about the case.

Instead they'd both signed forms giving her power of attorney, not only to act in Gino's name, but to be Marcello's and Sofia's guardian if Gino were absent.

However the greater portion of the time she sat listening to a detailed explanation of the vast assets and holdings of the entire Montefalco family.

"This document will go into effect the minute you become Gino's wife. It says, 'In the event of the untimely deaths or mental incapacities of both

Gino and Sofia, *you* will automatically become the Duchess of Montefalco."

Ally's gasp permeated the elegant law office. Her fingers shook so hard she couldn't hold the pen.

Beneath the conference table she felt Gino's hand slide to her thigh. It sent shock waves through her system. He squeezed gently.

"It's just a formality," he whispered.

She jerked her head around. "Is there something you haven't told me?" she cried. "Marcello's condition isn't hereditary is it?"

She couldn't stop the tremor in her voice.

Gino's surprised expression should have told her the answer to that question. But the thought of anything being wrong with him had upset her so much, she wasn't thinking rationally.

"I swear to you there's not a thing wrong with me or Sofia," came his solemn declaration.

Though she believed him, she couldn't prevent the shiver that ran through her body.

"Sign it, Ally, then this part will be over and I'll finally have peace of mind."

Knowing how vital it was for him to get his affairs in order at such a precarious time in their lives, she managed to write her name on the dotted line one more time.

When she laid down the pen, a haunting sigh escaped his lips, reminding her this was no game but a life and death situation.

Gino handed the document back to his attorney, then turned to Ally.

"With that out of the way we can enjoy our trip to Ischia."

"Ischia?" Mr. Toscano questioned.

"That's where I'm taking the family after the ceremony."

The older man shook his head.

"I'm afraid it's out of the question now, Gino. You could be arraigned at your farmhouse as early as this afternoon."

Ally let out a cry. "Surely not this soon—"

"Anything's possible, *signora*. If they have to track you to Naples and beyond, it could be ugly for Sofia."

"I don't want my niece hurt in any way," Gino muttered grimly.

"Neither do I," the attorney said. "But if the prosecutor decides you pose too much of a threat, he can order you brought in anytime he likes."

"How long will they keep him?" Ally tried without success to keep the alarm out of her voice.

"It could be anywhere from one to three days. Depending on the judge's findings, a trial date could be set. After that Gino will be released on his own recognizance, but he'll be under house arrest. That means both of you stay on the farm."

Ally rubbed her temples where they'd started to ache. "I had no idea it could happen this fast."

Mr. Toscano eyed her with compassion. "It may not happen today or tomorrow. It might not happen for another week. But I know how this prosecutor works. He's ambitious and hungry.

"It's crucial to this case that you two keep your marriage under wraps before he makes his first official move against either of you.

"Since you took out a special license yesterday, I'd advise you to get married right now."

"You're reading my mind," Gino murmured, pulling out his cell phone.

Her adrenaline gushed. "But how can we do that?"

The attorney spread his hands in an expansive gesture.

"Very easily, *signora*. The Montefalco name opens doors. You're welcome to use this conference room. Judge Mancini is just across the courtyard. There shouldn't be a problem of his stepping over here long enough to officiate. Shall I get him on the phone, Gino?"

Gino simply nodded because he was already talking to someone.

While both men were thus occupied, Ally's thoughts reeled.

The second Gino ended his call, she grasped his arm.

"What about Sofia? She's going to be devastated if we do this without her."

"Maybe not." His black eyes flashed her a searching glance.

"Barring another emergency, Father Angelini has agreed to be available at any time. If I'm not officially served this afternoon, he'll perform the ceremony at the church this evening."

"He would do that?"

"Of course. Either way it's the only plan to stay ahead of the prosecutor."

"Y-you're right," she whispered, but he was already making another call and probably didn't hear her response.

She tried to school her feelings. Tonight would be their wedding night...

Even if they wouldn't be sleeping together, Ally's heart pounded furiously.

After a few minutes of conversation, he hung up and looked at her.

"Provided nothing goes wrong, it's all arranged with Bianca and the staff for seven o'clock. Sofia and the girls can still wear the new dresses you picked out yesterday," Gino assured her. "The few people we've asked to attend will come just the same."

"What will you tell everyone is the reason for the change?"

"That I might have to go out of town on business at a moment's notice, and didn't want to wait any longer to make you mine. Our guests will understand."

He leaned over and kissed her warmly on the mouth.

She wished he hadn't done that. The world might not know the real reason they were getting married, but Mr. Toscano did.

Bemused by the way Gino made her feel every time his hands or mouth touched her, she got to her feet.

"If you'll excuse me, I'd like to use the powder room."

The attorney nodded. "It's down the hall to your right."

"Thank you."

Without looking at Gino she left the conference room, but he caught up to her and put a detaining hand on her upper arm. Warmth seeped through the material of her cream suit jacket to her skin.

"What's wrong, Ally?"

"I'm worried about Sofia's reaction when we tell her we'll have to postpone the trip."

That wasn't all Ally was thinking about, but her other thoughts were too private to share with him. "She was looking forward to going snorkeling."

"She understands when business calls. There'll be other times, Ally. I promise you that."

If it were humanly possible, Gino would always keep his word. But because someone had intentionally caused Jim and Donata's accident, the situation was out of their control.

And what if there'd been no accident?

Ally would have lived her whole life not knowing what happened to Jim.

I would never have met Gino…

She couldn't imagine not knowing him now. Such a possibility was beyond her comprehension.

The very thought of his going to prison when she loved him so desperately— It seemed happiness was going to elude her again.

Gino eyed her with concern, obviously unconvinced she'd told him everything. But she kept on walking, not daring to tell him the truth.

Twenty minutes later the young judge who appeared to be on friendly terms with Mr. Toscano pronounced them man and wife. It was a very brief to the point ceremony because he was in a hurry.

The obligatory kiss Gino gave her was brief but thorough.

"Congratulations, Signora Di Montefalco. It was an honor to officiate for you and the Duc."

The judge appeared duly impressed by Gino's title. She supposed Gino was the Duc until Sofia came of age. Incredible.

"May you both be very happy in your new life.

"If you and your beautiful bride will put your

signatures across from mine on the wedding certificate, my clerk will file it today."

Ally didn't think there was a wedding ceremony on record done with such dispatch.

It took family connections in high places that only someone of Gino's name and stature could arrange on a moment's notice.

When she'd signed her name, Gino put his arm around her shoulders and hugged her to him.

"Thank God for you," he whispered into her silken gold curls. "I swear on my parents' grave to do everything in my power to make certain you never regret this decision."

She lifted tremulous eyes to his. "I promise you the same thing, Gino."

"Let's go home," he murmured.

Home…

He kept his arm around her as they left the building and hurried to the parking area where Paolo was waiting.

He wasn't alone.

Ally pulled back. "What are those two men doing at your car?"

She heard Gino curse, even though he'd said it in Italian.

"Alberto must have been psychic. They've come to escort me to the magistrate's office for questioning. Poor Bianca must have been forced to tell them where I was."

No matter how much Ally wanted to scream at this injustice, she couldn't fall apart now. Gino needed her to be strong for him.

"We knew it was just a matter of time, Gino. I'm glad it happened here instead of the farm-house."

"So am I."

"I'll take care of everything. We'll have that church service for Sofia after you return."

Gino squeezed her hand with so much force she wanted to cry out, but she didn't because she knew he wasn't aware of his own strength. Not when he'd just been plunged into hell.

"Ally—" His dark eyes stared straight through to her soul. She knew what he was trying to say.

"Don't worry about anything. Go with them. The sooner you comply, the sooner you'll be back."

"Signore Di Montefalco?" They flashed their identity cards.

"Get in the car now," he whispered to Ally.

She rushed to do his bidding. The moment she closed the door, Paolo sped away.

She turned to look out the back window. To her horror she saw some paparazzi gathered on the pavement.

Flashes went off as the man who was bigger than life to her climbed into the back of an unmarked car with both men flanking him.

"Quickly, Paolo. I need to talk to Bianca on the phone."

"Si, signora."

He rang the farmhouse, then passed the cell phone to her.

"Bianca?" she cried when the housekeeper answered. "It's Ally. Listen very carefully."

She explained about them getting married in the attorney's office.

"It didn't happen any too soon. Gino has been arraigned."

The older woman's cry echoed her own.

"Whatever you do, don't tell Sofia anything. I'll talk to her myself the second I get home."

"I will say nothing, Ally. She and Anna are playing outside on the terrace with Rudolfo."

"Good. Keep them there. Thank you for everything. Paolo and I will be home shortly. Then you and I can make the necessary phone calls to Father Angelini and Gino's friends."

"Bene. May I say congratulations again, *signora.* I'm very happy for you and Gino. With you in the house, he won't be so worried about everything while he's gone."

"That's what I'm hoping. Bless you, Bianca."

After hanging up, she said, "Paolo? I've got lots of ideas to keep Sofia busy, but I'm going to need your help with some of them."

"I'm at your service."

"Is there a place in the garage where Sofia and I could separate some lavender into bundles to make small gifts?"

"I'll clear a place for you."

"That would be wonderful. On our way home, we need to stop at a store in Remo that sells cellophane paper and ribbon."

He gave another nod. "I know just the place where Gino has an account."

"Perfect. We also need to stop at a paint store."

"Anything you want."

Maybe it was too much to hope that she could keep Sofia in the dark while Gino was gone.

But with security in place around the farm, and help from the staff, Ally was determined that if at all possible, her new stepniece would be spared any more pain to do with Donata.

To Ally's relief, Sofia didn't see her arrive at the farmhouse when they drove in an hour later.

Bianca informed her Anna's father had come to get his daughter. For the time being Sofia was on a walk with her father and Roberto.

It gave Ally time to help Bianca make phone calls explaining that the wedding ceremony had to be postponed until Gino could get back from an important business trip.

With that done, Ally swallowed a late lunch. Before long Sofia returned with her father.

When the girl saw Ally, she put the cat down and

ran over to hug her. "I'm glad you and Uncle Gino are back, Anna, and I can't wait until tomorrow."

"I know exactly how you feel." She took a fortifying breath. "Would you believe some important business of your father's came up? Gino has to deal with it, so we're going to be married in a couple of days when he gets back."

Sofia's eyes filled on cue. "But everyone is planning on it tomorrow!"

"Your uncle called Anna's parents, and the Rossinis. It's all set for a few days from now. Father Angelini is standing by."

Sofia was doing her best not to break down. "When, exactly?"

"Maybe three days at the most. In the meantime, I thought you and I would get busy on several projects I have in mind to surprise Gino."

She wiped her eyes. Partially mollified, she asked, "What projects?"

"Well for one, I need you to teach me Italian. I want to be able to say some things to Gino in his language on our wedding day. I would like to speak with such an authentic accent, he'll be shocked. It'll be our secret of course."

The girl's brown eyes suddenly sparkled. "You mean like 'I love you'?"

"Exactly. Like, 'I can't live without you.' Like, 'you're the most wonderful man I've ever known.

Like, 'you're my heart and soul. Like 'I love your niece like my own daughter.'"

Sofia went perfectly quiet. "I love you, too, Ally. More than anything!"

"Then we're the luckiest people in the world."

"Gino?"

The second Gino heard Alberto's voice, he sprang from the hotel room bed where he'd spent the night going mad without a phone. His family's power may not have prevented him being investigated but did give him certain privileges.

Two security guards took turns bringing him meals, but there was no communication.

Today would be his second day before the chief judge while he made statements and listened to the prosecutor's charges against him.

The judge would decide if there was enough evidence to call for a trial.

So far it sounded even worse than Gino had first supposed.

Mercifully Alberto had come. He was the only person allowed in to talk to Gino.

Speaking in hushed tones his attorney said, "I've talked to your wife. All is well with her and Sofia for the moment."

Gino swallowed hard. "That's the kind of news I needed to hear."

"I only have a few minutes. Thanks to the

e-mails that placed Donata and her lover in the one location no one thought to look, those P.I.'s you hired to nose around Palermo, Sicily, have unearthed interesting news. It seems Donata had a great-aunt on the Castiglione side who's still alive and holds the purse strings to their family fortune."

Gino shot to his feet. "I don't think even Marcello knew about that, otherwise he would have told me."

Alberto eyed him shrewdly. "She probably kept that a secret from him like she did a lot of things. This aunt was the one who let Donata stay with her, and allowed her to use the family yacht.

"Apparently James Parker was a guest there and on the yacht several times. One of the crew let it out that the yacht picked them up in Portofino, Italy, but some members of the family weren't happy about it, particularly the great-aunt's oldest son named Vassily.

"He's next in line to inherit the money, and wouldn't stand for sharing it with a long lost family member from Rome like Donata who suddenly decided to ingratiate herself and her lover."

Gino's heart pounded like a jackhammer. His thoughts leaped ahead.

"This Vassily could have pretended to be Donata's friend by helping her procure that getaway car. All he had to do was pay off a couple of thugs to fix the brakes."

Alberto nodded. "Give the P.I.'s a little more time to investigate Vassily's activities, Gino. If everything adds up, we might well have our culprit."

Gino clapped his attorney on the shoulder. "Get all the extra help you need. I don't care how much it costs."

The other man nodded. "I'll tell your wife you're doing fine and should be home in another day or two."

"*Grazie*, Alberto."

"See you in chambers in a little while."

Ally stood in the alcove to Gino's bedroom with her hands on her hips. After dinner she and Sofia had come back with vases of fresh flowers to provide the finishing touch.

She and Sofia had spent most of yesterday painting the walls in both rooms a tan color with white trim. It covered the off-white paint which had probably been on the aged walls since the farmhouse was built.

"What do you think, Sofia?

"Uncle Gino's going to love it!"

"I hope so. That daybed and table from the storage room are a good fit."

Sofia nodded. "It looks a lot better than an empty nook. I guess Uncle Gino didn't know what to do with it."

"If he gave up his old room for you and your

father, then it makes sense he hasn't had time to worry about this suite of rooms. That's what wives are for," Ally quipped.

Sofia flashed her a mysterious smile.

"What's that look all about?"

"If you and Uncle Gino have a baby, this would make a sweet nursery."

"You're right," Ally said, trying to sound matter-of-fact.

"There's room for a crib," Sofia observed. "Signora Rossini has a new baby. Leonora tends it all the time. She says it's so much fun."

"What's so much fun?"

They both turned at the same time.

"Uncle Gino!" Sofia flew into his arms.

Ally's urge to do the same thing was so intense, she was in pain holding herself back.

He'd been gone three endless days. She'd given up hope he'd be home tonight.

He was still wearing the pale blue suit he'd been arraigned in, which meant he'd just been released and needed his suite to shower and change.

Ally thought he looked tired and leaner, yet all the more attractive for it.

"I was just telling Ally I hope you have a baby soon."

"What kind would you like? I'll see what I can do," he teased.

Heat swamped Ally's face.

"I don't care if it's a boy or a girl. Do you?"

"As long as the baby's healthy, I'll take whatever comes and be grateful."

"Me, too." She hugged Gino again.

"Do you like your surprise? Ally and I did all the painting ourselves. It's your welcome home present."

Ally saw his gaze take in the alcove's furnishings, but his eyes were hooded making it impossible to read their expression.

"I feel like I've just wandered into one of Rome's most fashionable furniture galleries."

Sofia laughed. "It was Ally's idea. Do you like the new matching bedspreads?"

They were a café-au-lait with white swirls.

He tousled his niece's hair. "I love them. They're classically modern. Did you pick them out?"

"We both thought this was the prettiest pattern. Ally said the daybed was perfect if you ever want Papa to be close to you during the night."

Gino's eyes swerved to Ally's. She noticed a strange flickering in their black depths. New sensations fired her blood.

"Ally is always concerned with everyone else's needs. That's why I'm marrying her first thing in the morning."

Sofia did a close approximation of squealing in delight.

"I made all the arrangements on the drive home from Rome. The ceremony will be at ten o'clock."

Ally rubbed her hands against her jean-clad hips, all the time aware of Gino's scrutiny.

"In that case I'll say good night to the two of you, Gino. It's already late, and I need my sleep for the big day ahead."

She sensed Gino had a lot to tell her, but now wasn't the time. She didn't want anything to alarm Sofia this close to the wedding.

Sofia ran over to her and gave her a big hug. "Good night, Ally. I can't wait for morning to come."

Neither could Ally.

"I feel the same way." She kissed the girl's cheek, then hurried out of the bedroom.

His suite was located at one end of the third floor.

She went down the stairs to her room on the second. Sofia's and her father's suite lay at the other end of the hall.

Before Gino had been forced to move his family here, he'd had the farmhouse for himself. By virtue of taking on a wife, he'd now been invaded.

She hoped he didn't mind what she'd done upstairs. They already had an understanding that they'd be sleeping apart. She just didn't want him to think she planned to turn his whole household upside down.

When she could talk to him alone, she would

explain that she felt this had been a good way to keep Sofia's spirits up, and accomplish what needed to be done without anyone questioning her real motives.

But once under the covers of her own bed, her mind wouldn't shut off.

What a difference it made knowing Gino was home. His mere presence gave her an overwhelming feeling of contentment.

Growing up in an all woman household, Ally had never known such luxury.

Something about Gino engendered this marvelous feeling of well-being and security. She knew he would slay dragons for them.

How odd that Jim hadn't had this same effect on her. Physically he'd been a strong, capable man. But she must have recognized instinctively he would always put himself first. In the end, he did it to his own demise.

Gino was a different breed of man altogether. No one else measured up.

She couldn't believe she was his wife. Even if it was in name only, she vowed to be his equal in all the ways that counted.

After the ceremony tomorrow, she would call her mother on Gino's cell phone and tell her she was married.

Much as she would have liked her mother's blessing, she hadn't needed it to function.

It was all because of Gino.

As for Jim's parents, depending on many factors, she would phone to inform them she had remarried. But for the time being it would be bett—

"Ally?" Gino whispered in the darkness, jarring her out of her thoughts.

Surprised to hear his voice, she raised up on one elbow. "I didn't hear you knock."

In the next breath she felt her side of the mattress dip to take his weight.

"I hope you don't mind."

Her heart was pounding in her ears. "No. Of course not."

He was sitting so close, she could smell the soap he'd used in the shower. She started to move to give him room, but he stopped her by placing both hands on either side of her pillow, forcing her to lie back.

He was wearing a robe, and as far as she could tell, little else.

"You ran from my bedroom so fast, we didn't have a chance to talk."

Her breathing had grown shallow. "Sofia needed you."

He traced the curve of her jaw with his finger. "But my wife didn't?"

"That isn't what I meant," she whispered.

"Then what did you mean?" His fingers had trailed to her earlobe, turning her bones to liquid.

"I—I've been sick with worry waiting for you to come home and tell me everything. But I didn't want to let on in front of Sofia."

"You've done a magnificent job of keeping her occupied. I've never seen her this happy before. Now it's my turn."

"I don't understand."

"I've spent two hellish nights away from my wife. I'm not prepared to be alone tonight.

"Let me lie here. It's all I ask. I need my best friend."

She heard a strange nuance in his voice. An impending sense of dread took over.

"Something's wrong—" she cried in alarm. "What is it? Don't tell me it's nothing because I wouldn't believe you. Hasn't the investigation uncovered anything that will help our side?"

"They have several promising leads."

"But?"

His fingers tugged on one of her curls. "There's been a new twist in the case."

Moving with the stealth of a panther, he reached the end of the bed. Before she knew it, he'd come to lie on top of the comforter next to her. She felt him cover his forehead with his arm.

Making love to her had to be the furthest thing from his mind. She felt so stupid for even imagining that's what he'd had on his mind when he'd first come into her room unannounced.

They were two people intrinsically linked to a murder, fighting for survival. Gino had no one but her to turn to for the kind of mental comfort he craved. She was the only person who understood what he was going through.

Three days ago she'd vowed to comfort him for better or worse. This was definitely the worst time of their lives.

She turned so she was facing him. "Tell me what's happened," she urged softly.

In the intimacy of the darkness he began talking.

"There's going to be a trial. It has been set for a month from now."

Even though Ally knew it might come to this, the news was shattering.

"I just found out Merlina of all people is a witness for the prosecution."

Ally quivered inwardly, but she was determined to stay on an even keel for him.

"Did you meet her through Donata?"

"No. Merlina's father is a wholesale florist from Gubbio. I met her almost a year ago while she was helping her father.

"We went out several times, but I lost interest and told her it was over, By that time Donata's long vacations were starting to take their toll on Sofia. Comforting her was all I had on my mind."

"But Merlina didn't want to stop seeing you," Ally said out loud.

"No. She started coming to Remo once a month. She would show up at the flower stand waiting for me. I told her my life was complicated, and we could only be friends. I hoped she would give up without my having to spell it out to her."

Listen to what he's saying, Ally. Just listen, and learn.

"Without my knowledge, it seems she got in contact with Donata."

"Sofia told me she came to see her mother."

Gino groaned. "During those conversations Donata told lies about me. She made me out to be a dangerous man capable of committing bodily harm."

Ally was horrified. "Like what specifically?"

"According to the prosecutor, she told Merlina I used to come to her room at the palazzo and force myself on her because Marcello could no longer protect her."

"That's sick," Ally cried.

His breathing had become labored. "Donata showed Merlina the bruises to prove it."

Ally sat straight up in the bed. "Gino—if Merlina had believed Donata's lies, she would never have shown up here in the last few days. What reason did she use for coming to the farmhouse after all this time?"

"She wanted to know why I'd really stopped

seeing her. I told her what I'd said before. That it was over, and it wouldn't be fair to go on seeing her.

"But she refused to accept it. And then of course she saw you, Ally. She knew you were a guest in the house."

Ally moaned in disgust. "So she put two and two together, and in her jealous rage she decided to pay you back by running to the prosecutor with more lies."

"As Alberto keeps reminding me, her story won't be believed. Her credibility will be ruined when he gets her on the witness stand and it's learned she came to see me after Donata had warned her off. Nevertheless I have to admit I didn't see that one coming."

"Of course not. It's awful. I'd say it's a miracle you trust anyone." Her voice shook.

"You're it, Ally."

Her heart went out to him.

"You sound exhausted. Go to sleep."

After a few minutes she could tell he'd passed out from fatigue.

For the rest of the night she guarded him. When it grew cooler in the room, she stole out of bed to get an extra blanket from the cupboard. She put it over him.

Without conscious thought she smoothed the hair from his brow where his forearm had disheveled it.

Even the man she'd likened to Apollo needed respite from his burdens.

Toward morning she fell asleep and knew nothing until Sofia knocked on her door.

Ally's first thought was Gino. She opened her eyes to discover he'd left her bed already. She hadn't even noticed. Some guard she'd make.

"Come in, Sofia."

Her brunette head peeked around the door. "Uncle Gino says to hurry and get up. It's eight-thirty. Almost time to leave for the church."

"I slept that late?"

"After all the work you've been doing, he said you deserved to sleep in. He says he's so excited to get married, he can't eat."

After what he'd revealed to Ally in the darkness of the night, she wasn't surprised he'd lost his appetite.

"Have you eaten already?"

"Yes. With Papa. Now I'm going to get dressed."

"Okay. I'll hurry. Meet you downstairs in twenty minutes."

She threw off the covers and padded into the bathroom for a quick shower and shampoo.

After putting on new underwear, she went over to the closet.

For the wedding she'd picked out a two-piece suit in pale pink with a lace overlay on the short sleeved jacket.

The knee length chiffon skirt floated around her legs.

She fastened the tiny pearl buttons, before slipping into matching pale pink high heels. A pink frost on her lips, plus a poof of floral spray, and she was ready.

Gino stood waiting at the bottom of the stairs in a black tuxedo.

Once again an image flashed before her eyes of the fierce bodyguard who'd stepped from the wall into her life one dark night.

Who would have guessed the gorgeous, enigmatic stranger wearing a security guard's uniform would turn out to be her husband dressed in impeccable groom's attire?

Ally grew weak at the sight of so much male beauty.

As she reached the bottom step, he drew close. She heard him murmur something under his breath in Italian. She would have given anything to know what he said.

"A certain young, upcoming violinist told me these would match your suit."

From behind his back he produced a corsage of pink roses he pinned to her jacket.

Her heart thumped so hard, it caused the petals to rustle with each beat.

"If you hadn't been there for me last night, I swear I don't know what I would have done."

"I didn't do anything, Gino," she whispered shakily.

He kissed her forehead. "You believed in me from the beginning. Knowing that, I can get through this."

His trust in her was absolute. He didn't need anything else. Unfortunately she wanted and needed much more from him. But to behave like Donata and Merlina, neither of whom could take Gino's rejection, would be the kiss of death.

After tonight she was more convinced than ever she'd done the right thing by having a certain inscription engraved on the gold wedding band she'd bought him.

He'd wanted a best friend for a wife. That's what he was getting. She would have to find a way to live with the pain.

CHAPTER NINE

FATHER ANGELINI smiled at both of them. "And now I pronounce you Rudolfo Giannino Fioretto Di Montefalco, and you Allyson Cummings Parker, husband and wife. May you live long and be fruitful. In the name of the Father, the Son and the Holy Ghost, Amen."

Gino didn't hesitate to give her another thorough kiss in front of the small assembly of friends. They were now officially married in the eyes of the church.

In the periphery, Ally caught sight of Sofia's shining face. She and the girls looked adorable in white lace dresses with garlands of pink roses in their hair.

Marcello might have been in a wheelchair, but he looked every inch the aristocrat in his formal attire. He wore the crest of the Montefalco family on the scarlet band stretching from his right shoulder to his left hip.

Before Ally had started down the aisle of the church on Dizo Rossini's arm, his wife Maria had handed her a sheaf of long stemmed pink roses to carry.

"Do you know how many of my country women could claw your eyes out for getting Gino to marry you not once, but twice?" she teased.

Ally chuckled, but little did Maria know her bittersweet remark made Ally want to laugh and cry at the same time.

When the wedding party congregated on the steps of the church, one of Gino's friends took pictures for them.

Everything seemed so normal and happy, but Ally knew they were living on borrowed time. Like a bomb ticking away, their lives could be shattered by an explosion if Gino didn't win his case.

"Stop worrying," he whispered against her neck after they'd climbed in the back seat of the car.

"I'm not."

"Yes you are," came the no nonsense rejoinder. "I can tell by your eyes. They're a dark green. When you're happy, they turn a lighter shade and shimmer. Today is ours to enjoy."

She bowed her head. "I want to enjoy it, but I keep remembering those men waiting for you outside Mr. Toscano's office. If that were to happen in front of Sofia and all your friends—"

"No one's going to snatch me away again. That part is over."

Unless he was found guilty at the trial and taken away in handcuffs.

At the mere thought of it, Ally shuddered in horror.

"Where's my Joan of Arc who stood calmly before her enemies at the jail without as much as the quiver of an eyelash."

His question gave her a needed jolt. She'd better start acting the part she'd committed to play for life.

She raised her blond head. "I'm right here."

He grasped her hand. "I haven't told you how exquisite you look yet."

"Thank you."

"I'm the envy of all my friends."

"I have a few friends who would think the same about you."

When he kissed her fingers, she wanted to pull her hand away. How could she possibly remain friends with him if he kept doing things to remind her he was irresistible yet untouchable flesh and blood husband?

"I'm sorry your friends and family couldn't be here, Ally. One day our home will be open to everyone, and we'll be able to travel to Oregon."

"Sofia keeps asking me how soon you'll take us to see Mount Hood, Gino. She's fascinated by volcanoes."

"Aren't we all."

He slid his arm behind her shoulders. "I'm anxious to meet your mother and tell her what an exceptional daughter she has."

"You're going to come as a tremendous surprise to her."

"Is that good or bad," he mocked in a playful tone.

"I'm not going to bother answering that question. Suffice it to say that with my father's defection, my mother has lost her trust in men. But when she gets to really know you, her whole attitude will change."

"Trust is everything," he said in an emotion filled voice.

Ally already knew that. She stirred in place. "I agree."

Though she wanted to rest her head against his shoulder, she didn't dare for fear she'd give herself away.

"Before we left the church, Sofia told me to examine my ring carefully. I think I'll do it now."

He removed his arm in order to pull off his own ring.

Ally held her breath while she waited for his reaction.

"My kingdom for a friend," he read the words aloud.

After a breathless moment of quiet, he touched the ring to his lips, then slid it back on his finger.

By now they'd reached the courtyard of the farmhouse. Most of the guests had already arrived. More pictures were being taken.

Gino got out of the car and came around to help her. His black eyes resembled smoldering embers.

"In case you didn't know it, you've made me the happiest man alive."

Before she could take another breath, his mouth descended on hers. Like the effect of slow moving magma, it caught every particle of her body on fire.

Not until one of his friends shouted for Gino to keep on kissing her for the camera did Ally realize how carried away she'd gotten. Her husband couldn't have helped but be aware of her hungry response. She could only hope that since he was playing to the crowd, he assumed she was doing the same thing.

He pretended to be the amorous lover to such perfection, no one could have guessed the real reason for their marriage.

Everyone clapped. There were a few wolf whistles that brought a grin to Gino's handsome face. He ushered her inside the farmhouse where Bianca and some local helpers had arranged food and champagne in the dining room.

The guests filled their plates and wandered out to the back terrace where a group played music.

Without hesitation Gino pulled her into his arms and started dancing with her.

Soon others joined in. Eventually his friends broke in to dance with her, depriving her of the joy of being that close to him.

But she needn't have worried who Gino's next partners would be.

He gave each flower girl a turn around the patio before spending the rest of his time with Sofia.

Ally finally excused herself to spell off Luigi and Roberto, both of whom were there to help with Gino's brother and celebrate.

"I'll watch Marcello while you get something to eat," she told them.

When they got up, she grasped Marcello's hand in case he decided to start walking around the terrace.

Maybe it was the music, or the presence of so many people, but his thumb kept pressing the top of her hand.

She hoped it meant that in some obscure way he was enjoying himself.

The cruelty of his affliction made it hard on everyone who loved him. He and Gino had been exceptionally close.

Today should have been a time for the two brothers to rejoice.

But of course it would have been a happy time because Gino would have married someone else. A pain seared her heart to imagine missing out on marrying him.

"Ally?" Her husband appeared out of nowhere and put his hand on her arm. "What's made you go pale?"

"Did I? Maybe it's because I was wishing I'd known Marcello before he became ill."

His dark eyes flickered. "He would have been crazy about you even before he heard you play the Tchaikovsky."

"Do you know he's been pressing his thumb against my hand?"

He slanted her a mysterious glance that caused her pulse to race.

"He senses your kindness. Would you be as kind to me if I asked you to play something for our guests? I want to show you off, and I can't think of a present I'd like more on my wedding day."

"Gino—"

"Is that a yes, a no, or a maybe."

His charm made it impossible for her to refuse him anything.

When she thought of all he'd given her, it was so little to ask in return. But he had no idea how full her emotions were. They threatened to overpower her.

"Well, perhaps one piece."

"I'll ask my niece to bring out your violin."

He disappeared just as Luigi and Roberto came back on the terrace.

Soon a smiling Sofia walked over to her with her case.

The background music ended and Gino asked for everyone's attention.

"Ally and I want to thank you for sharing the most important day of our lives with us.

"Few of you know she's a gifted musician. I've asked her to play something for you as a special favor to me and my brother.

"Our parents instilled the love of music in us. Now we have Ally to fill the house with it again."

His touching words made Ally want to burst into tears.

To fight them off, she opened her case and tuned her violin until she felt she was in control once more.

"I'll play something from the Brahm's First Symphony."

Brahms was her favorite composer, whether it be piano or orchestral music.

This was the piece she'd been practicing when the migraine had hit her so hard during rehearsal in Portland. Little had she known what awaited her when she'd gone out in the hall to call the doctor and discovered there was another message waiting.

In a matter of weeks that voice mail from Troy had literally transformed her life.

Here she was in the heart of the Italian countryside, playing at her own wedding for her brand-new husband. The man she loved beyond comprehension.

For a little while she simply immersed herself in the beauty of the piece, wanting it to please Gino.

When she finished playing, there was an unnatural quiet.

Perhaps the greatest tribute to any artist was the hushed silence that followed a performance.

She looked across the patio and met Gino's gaze. Even from the distance separating them, his eyes seemed to be aflame.

Suddenly he began to applaud. Soon the others followed his lead.

"Grazie," he mouthed the words to her before she was besieged by their guests.

Sofia clung to her hand and announced she was taking lessons. That brought on requests from several parents for Ally to teach their children.

Everyone asked for an encore but to her relief Gino came to the rescue.

"I don't want my bride worn-out before the wedding day is over."

His remarks incited the men to make their little jokes. Ally didn't need a translator to know they were talking about the pleasures of the wedding night to come.

She laughed along with them because they were among friends here and Gino needed a moment like this to get him through the dark days of the trial coming up.

While she was putting her violin back in the case, she felt a pair of strong arms slide around her waist.

"Leave the violin on the chair and dance with me again."

Ally's heart leaped in response. It was frightening how much she wanted to be in Gino's arms. But this couldn't go on much longer or he would know he'd married a woman who wanted to be much more than friends.

Avoiding his eyes, she followed his lead. He seemed determined to show his friends that he was in love with his wife. Ally had to withstand his wrapping both arms around her with his hands splayed across her back, his face pressed into her curls.

Unlike the other couples, he more or less moved them in place. You really couldn't call it dancing. She could feel every hard line and sinew of his body.

Desire like she'd never known in her life engulfed her. She felt the telltale weakness in her limbs. Her palms ached with pain only he could assuage.

She couldn't do this any longer.

Placing her hands against his chest, she pushed away a little, but not so anyone else would notice.

Still not looking at him she said, "I'm sorry, Gino, but I need to be excused for a minute."

"Of course. Hurry back." He gave her mouth a lingering kiss before letting her go.

The mere contact set off a conflagration inside her.

In a daze, she made her way through the crowded house to the hallway. As she started up the stairs she saw Bianca welcome another guest into the foyer. Ally didn't recognize the middle-aged man. He hadn't been at the church to witness the ceremony.

If the housekeeper hadn't greeted him like an old friend, Ally would have been terrified it was someone from the prosecutor's office.

She continued up the stairs to her room to freshen up in the bathroom. In truth she'd needed to get away from Gino.

Ally soaked a washcloth in cold water and pressed it to her hot face, surprised she didn't hear it sizzle.

Her biggest mistake had been to dance with him. When she went downstairs again, she would make certain it didn't happen again. That way she might just be able to make it through her wedding day without the whole world knowing how she felt about Gino.

A few minutes later she felt settled down enough to leave her room and rejoin their guests.

To her surprise she almost collided with a white-faced Sofia who'd been running from the direction of her own bedroom further down the hall.

"Sofia—what is it? Has something happened to your father?"

"No." In the next breath the girl's expression closed up. She started for the stairs, but Ally pulled her back and held on to her.

"Was someone mean to you?"

"No."

"Then what's wrong, darling? Don't you know you can tell me or your uncle anything?"

"I don't like Uncle Gino anymore," came her muffled cry against Ally's lace jacket.

Sick to the pit of her stomach, Ally drew Sofia into the bedroom and shut the door.

She walked her over to the bed and helped her to sit down next to her.

Though they had a house full of guests downstairs, this was a problem that needed to be taken care of right now.

"Why do you feel that way about Gino? He loves you so much."

"I know."

The girl was talking in riddles.

"What's upset you? Please tell me. You can trust me."

"I'm afraid to tell you." She burst into tears. "It would hurt you too much."

"Hurt me? How?"

"Because you love him. But he—" She couldn't go on.

"He what?" Ally prodded.

"It'll make you cry."

"Then we'll cry together. Tell me."

"I found out he wishes—he wishes—" She couldn't say it. Breaking into half sobs, she clung blindly to Ally who by this time feared this had something to do with Donata. Ally couldn't let this go.

"Please, Sofia. You can't keep this to yourself or it will make you ill."

Sofia finally raised her head. "He said he wished he hadn't married you, but it was the only thing he could do at the time."

It was one thing for Ally to know the truth in her own heart, but to hear Gino's niece say it was like undergoing a second death.

Fighting to remain calm Ally said, "Is that what he told you?"

"No." She kept wiping her eyes. "I heard him talking to Signore Santi."

"When?"

"Just now."

"You mean they're in your father's room?" It had to have been the man who'd come late to the reception.

"Yes. When I saw them leave the party and you

weren't downstairs, I came up to see what was going on. That's when I heard Signore Santi tell Uncle Gino it was too bad he married you when it wasn't necessary."

Not necessary— Did that mean there'd been a break in the case?

"Then U-Uncle Gino said—well you know what he said. I—I couldn't believe he said that."

Sofia's shoulders shook with silent sobs. "I thought he loved you."

Poor Sofia had been caught up in the romance, but cruel reality had intruded.

"Did you hear anything else?"

"No. I didn't want Uncle Gino to know I was listening."

Thank heaven for that!

Ally's arms closed around her. "Your secret is safe with me."

The girl lifted her tearstained face. "I shouldn't have told you. Now you'll go away and I'll never see you again." Her voice throbbed.

"That's not true, Sofia. I'm going to live right here with you forever.

"The fact that he doesn't love me doesn't change my love for him or you."

"How can you say that?"

"Listen to me, darling. When your uncle proposed, I knew he didn't love me. We're friends you see? So you mustn't stop loving him. He can't help how he feels. But I know he'll always be kind to me. He wants us to be a happy family. So do I."

Sofia studied her for a long time. "I love you, Ally. Do you think someday I could call you Mama?"

The question melted Ally's heart.

She winked at her. "As long as I can refer to you as my daughter, you can start calling me that anytime you like. Now wash your face and we'll go downstairs before everyone starts to wonder what has happened to the wedding party."

Alone for a moment, Ally squared her shoulders.

Where Gino's feelings were concerned, she hadn't learned anything from Sofia that she didn't already know. The difference was, realizing Sofia knew it, too, would make things much easier around here.

When Sofia emerged from the bathroom, Ally grasped her hand.

"After we leave this room, we'll pretend we never had this conversation, agreed?"

"Yes," she answered in a sober tone.

But it was easier said than done. When they joined their guests, Gino still hadn't come downstairs. That as much as anything let her know something of tremendous import had happened, otherwise Gino wouldn't absent himself from the festivities this long.

For Gino's sake she hoped Signore Santi's arrival meant that Gino was no longer under suspicion.

How would they go on protecting Sofia if there were a trial and he had to leave the farm every day to be in court?

She was an intelligent girl and no one's fool. Ally feared it was going to be sooner than later that she learned the whole ugly truth about her mother. Then it would come out that Ally's first husband had died with Donata.

Ally dreaded the day Sofia knew everything.

After urging Sofia to be with her friends, Ally mingled with the guests who were all enjoying themselves.

Ally caught up with Maria and talked to her about the possibility of Ally and Sofia helping out part-time at the flower stand for the rest of the summer.

Maria couldn't have been more enthused over the idea. They agreed to talk about it in a few days.

"Provided Gino is willing to share you by then."

To Ally's surprise Gino reappeared. He slid his arm around her waist.

"I saw your heads together. What plot are you two hatching behind my back?"

Ally wanted to ask him the same question about his conversation with Signore Santi who was nowhere in sight.

"Your wife and Sofia are going to come to work at the stand this summer."

"Provided you agree," Ally said to him.

She felt his probing glance.

"You'd really like to sell flowers?"

"I'd love it. So would Sofia. She'll help me with my Italian."

"Leonora will be overjoyed," Maria assured her.

His arm hugged her a little tighter. "My wife lights her own fires. She's out of my sight for five minutes, and already we're a farming family."

"It's what you always wanted, Gino. I couldn't be happier for both of you."

"Thank you, Maria." He kissed her cheek. "Now if you don't mind, I'm going to whisk my bride away to a secret place."

He guided Ally toward the hallway.

"We'll slip out the side door of the kitchen," he murmured against her ear.

She swallowed hard. "What about Sofia?"

"Anna's parents are keeping her with them tonight."

"Does Sofia know that?"

"I told her before I came to find you."

"W-was she all right with it?"

"Of course. She's old enough to know a wedding couple needs time to themselves."

He swept her out the door to the courtyard where Paolo was waiting with the car.

"Where are we going?"

"The palazzo."

"I thought we couldn't leave the farm."

"Legally we're not supposed to. But Carlo Santi came to the reception with news that necessitates a visit there. Since it's our wedding night, he's taking the responsibility of vouching for us while we break the rules."

Now everything made sense. This was a charade for Gino's friends in order to perpetuate the pretense of the happily married couple going off on their honeymoon.

By the time they started to pull away from the courtyard, their guests had assembled to see them off.

Ally exchanged a soulful glance with Sofia who ran out in front of everyone who were taking pictures to wave. She was on the verge of tears.

"Gino—we can't leave Sofia behind. Look at her face."

"I've seen it, but she's better off with friends until we return."

Ally knew he was right, but it hurt to leave her when Ally knew his niece was suffering since overhearing Gino's talk with Carlo.

"We'll be in Montefalco shortly. When we start the climb up the road to the west gate, we'll lower our heads to avoid the paparazzi camped nearby. I'm phoning ahead to tell the guards to have the gate open for us. That way Paolo won't have to stop."

Ally waited until he'd used his cell phone

before asking, "How long are you going to keep me in suspense about the case?"

He reached for her hand. His eyes flashed her a fiery glance. In the next few minutes he told her about the information uncovered by the P.I.'s in Sicily.

"One of the crew of the yacht has claimed that the great-aunt's grandson, Tomaso, has villas in Prague and Portofino. It seems he became friendly with Donata and your husband.

"It's possible he knows something about the accident, or even caused it. But without some sort of proof, it's the crewman's word against a wealthy member of the Castiglione family.

"In four months the authorities investigating this case haven't ever found evidence linking Donata and your husband. But you and I know the laptop exists. Which means Donata had to use some sort of computer on her end. "The fact that the authorities don't know of the correspondence between them plays to our advantage.

"Both Carlo and Alberto think she must have kept one at the palazzo, but it was hidden so well, the police never came across it.

"Naturally they went over Marcello's computer as part of the initial investigation, but nothing turned up.

"That's why I originally had my P.I.'s looking in all the coffee houses with computers in and around

St. Mortiz, hoping to discover she'd used one of them. Unfortunately they never found anything."

Ally sucked in her breath. "Then let's tear the palazzo apart."

"That's the idea," Gino muttered. "Maybe we'll find it. If she had someone like Tomaso helping her, that information has to be somewhere. She couldn't have carried out everything without help from someone she thought she could trust.

"It's the kind of proof needed to take to the chief judge. It will force him to consider other suspects."

"We'll spend all night if we have to," she declared.

Not only could it mean Gino's freedom, but she'd be spared having to go to his room with him in order to fool the staff that the newlyweds couldn't wait to be alone.

She stared out the passenger window. They were near the town now. She checked her watch. It was only five in the afternoon. The sun wouldn't be setting for hours yet.

"Wouldn't it have been better to arrive in one of the estate cars with the smoked glass?"

Gino shook his head. "That's a dead giveaway. The paparazzi won't be expecting a car I use at the farm. It will buy us the time we need to make it inside the grounds."

A few minutes later Paolo muttered that they'd better get down.

Gino reached for Ally and pulled her over so the top portion of her body lay against his hard thighs.

When she was settled, he leaned over her where she could feel his heart pounding against her back.

"Am I crushing you, Ally?"

"No. I'm fine."

"I knew my beautiful bride would say that," he whispered. "Hold on. The car's picking up speed. You won't have to suffer much longer."

That depended on the kind of suffering he was referring to. She had a lifetime of it ahead of her, but it would remain a secret between her and Sofia.

Suddenly the car came to a stop. Paolo gave the all clear.

Gino kissed Ally's brow as she raised up. "By now you have to know I'd rather be with you than anyone else in a situation like this."

She knew…

He came around to her side and opened the door. "Let's go in and get busy."

The palazzo was an eighteenth century palace so fabulous in its architectural beauty as well as its furnishings, Ally followed Gino around in awe.

He introduced her to the staff who congratulated them on their marriage. She could tell they held Gino in the greatest affection.

"We'll go to my apartment first and change."

"I don't have any of my clothes with me."

"You can wear something of mine."

He led her up marble stairs and through marble hallways to his apartment on the second floor. It was a fabulous home within a home where he could be totally self-contained.

Ally had thought his farmhouse was out of this world. But this kind of splendor left her speechless.

He pulled a pair of clean navy sweats from one of the drawers and handed them to her.

"Go ahead and use the bathroom while I change in here. Then we'll get started in Donata's dayroom where she spent a lot of time."

Once inside the large, modernized bathroom, Ally took off her wedding outfit and hung it on the door hook.

After removing her high heels, she put on Gino's clothes. They pretty well drowned her, but it was all right because she rolled up the sleeves. The elastic at the bottom of the legs kept her from tripping.

She padded back in the suite in her nylons.

He'd put on a pair of gray sweats. When he saw her he grinned.

"We look like a pair of athletes ready for a run."

Her mouth curved in a half smile. "I'm glad we'll be doing it inside here, or my poor feet couldn't take it."

His gaze traveled down her curvaceous body. "New shoes are the price of looking gorgeous on your wedding day."

"It was a wonderful day, Gino. Thank you for everything. Now let's see what we can find."

A half hour later they'd searched every square inch of the elegant dayroom on the main floor without success. Lines darkened his features. She hated to see him like that.

"I've been thinking. If I were Donata and wanted to hide something, I think I would have put it in Sofia's room."

His jaw hardened. "The police searched it thoroughly."

"But they weren't necessarily looking for a computer of some kind."

"You're right."

"Of course there's always the possibility she didn't own one, but had access through a friend."

"We'll take one last look anyway," Gino murmured.

Sofia's bedroom was across the hall from Marcello and Donata's apartment at the other end of the second floor.

"If Donata wanted to send messages, it would have been easy enough for her to slip across the hall when Sofia was at a friend's house or at school,' he said before ushering her inside his niece's room.

Ally felt like she'd entered the domain of a princess.

Her glance fell on the floor to ceiling bookcase with all kinds of books, puzzles and games.

"A laptop isn't so easily disguised, Gino. My guess is, if Donata had one, she camouflaged it in some way."

Gino shot her a piercing regard. "You're a woman with amazing instincts. Where would *you* hide it, Ally?"

She examined everything in sight.

"What's in that chest at the foot of Sofia's bed?"

"It has a lot of her toys in it. When Donata wanted to get rid of them, Marcello insisted on keeping them in case they ever had another baby."

She walked over to it. "The police probably did a cursory search, but toy boxes are notorious for holding treasures you never expect to find."

Ally opened the lid. It was a deep rectangular piece of furniture.

Gino got down on his haunches next to her and they began sifting through the jumble of items. When her hands came in contact with something about the right size, Ally let out a little cry of excitement.

But she soon groaned at the sight of a play typewriter in a plastic case.

"I was so sure—"

Gino went back to searching. She dug in at the other end and found a doctor's kit. Gino produced a makeup kit.

Starting to lose hope, she felt around the bottom. Her fingers came in contact with what she presumed was a radio in a leather case. Out of curiosity, she opened it.

A gasp came out of her. "Gino—this looks like a palm pilot! Do you think it's real?"

He took it from her and pressed the on button.

"It's real all right," his voice grated. "State-of-the-art four gig drive. Ally—" He crushed her against him. "You found it!"

She pulled away from him, unable to take much more of their physical contact.

"Get inside it quick!" she cried.

He helped her up from the floor. By tacit agreement they sat down on the side of Sofia's canopy bed.

The next five minutes felt like five hours as Gino started retrieving messages. Suddenly his tall, powerful body sprang from the bed.

"This says it all, Ally. Tomaso was the one to arrange for the car from a garage in St. Moritz. It names the place and the mechanic who let Donata buy the used car off him. Everything's there. The plan for them to drive to Portofino and board the yacht on January 25.

"Ally—" His eyes blazed with light. "Come on."

He grasped her hand. "We'll go to Marcello's study and phone our attorney."

Ally's gaze swerved to his. "If Signore Toscano needs an affidavit from Troy, I know he'll cooperate. It will prove the connection beyond any doubt."

Gino nodded. "You cracked the case wide-open, Ally. What would I have done if you hadn't come to Italy with your husband's laptop?"

Ally was euphoric to realize the horrible nightmare would soon be over. Whoever had tampered with those brakes, it wasn't Gino!

But because Ally had flown to Italy, Gino was now a married man, tied for life to a woman he would always consider his best friend.

But she couldn't imagine a virile man like him remaining celibate for that long. There was only one thing to do. She would talk to him about it after they'd returned to the farmhouse.

CHAPTER TEN

GINO got out of the car and hurried into the farm-house.

"Ally?"

Bianca came rushing into the foyer. "She's doing errands in the truck."

He frowned. "Is Sofia with her?"

"No. She got home a little while ago and is upstairs with her father."

Gino could scarcely contain his disappointment. Not with the news he had to tell her. He'd asked Ally to be here when he got home.

Last night Alberto had told Gino to come to Rome and they'd work all night to present their case before the chief judge. Carlo had gone with him.

It was decided Paolo would drive Ally back to the farmhouse. Gino had assured her they'd celebrate today. He'd been living for it and couldn't imagine where she'd gone. But Sofia would know.

He took the steps three at a time and hurried toward Marcello's suite.

The last thing he expected to find was his niece sobbing her heart out on her father's lap.

"Sofia?" he called to her.

She lifted her head. "Hello, Uncle Gino."

Normally she came running to him.

"What's wrong, sweetheart?"

"Nothing," she answered in a dull voice.

Gino's eyes met Luigi's. The nurse shrugged his shoulders, indicating he didn't know the reason for her tears.

"Let's go in your room and have a talk."

"I'd rather not."

He felt like someone had just kicked him in the gut.

"If something happened at Anna's house, I need to know about it."

"This isn't about Anna."

"Are you upset with me for asking you to spend the night at her house?"

"No." She wiped her eyes.

"Did you and Ally have words?" He couldn't fathom it, but he had to know the truth.

"No. I love her. She said I could call her Mama."

Though those words thrilled him, he still didn't have his answer.

"Then there's something I've done to hurt you. If I did, you know I didn't mean to."

"I know."

"Then I *have* hurt you. If you don't tell me what I've done, then I don't know how to fix it."

"You can't fix it." She sounded like a woman three times her age.

He'd never seen Sofia behave like this before. His body broke out in a cold sweat.

"Why do you say that?"

"Because it's true."

"Then I've failed you, Sofia, and that devastates me."

He left the room and went upstairs. How could the joy of this day be trumped by the pain he was feeling now?

The fact that Ally wasn't here caused him to wonder if she'd left on purpose so he and Sofia could be alone to sort things out.

Was it possible his niece had learned the truth about her mother, and believed Gino was guilty of driving Donata away? The very thought made him so ill, he staggered over to his bed, wondering how in the hell to help Sofia if he was right.

He could provide the proof that he wasn't the culprit. But he couldn't do anything about Sofia's deep seated sorrow where her mother was concerned. If she knew it was Ally's husband who'd died with her, Sofia would feel so betrayed, she'd never get over it.

Ally—where are you?

In his agony, he heard a rap on the door and raced across the room to fling it open and embrace his wife.

It was his niece.

"Sofia—"

"Can I come in?"

"What do you think?"

He could thank God she was at least speaking to him.

"Ally told me not to blame you because you couldn't help it."

"Blame me for what, sweetheart?"

She stared at him for the longest time. "I heard you talking to Signore Santi in Papa's room during the reception."

Gino replayed their conversation in his mind.

"What exactly did you hear?"

"He said something about you not having to get married after all. And you said—you said you wished you hadn't gotten married, but it was the only thing you could do at the time."

Gino had been holding his breath. "And from that you deduced that I don't love Ally. Is that it?"

She nodded slowly.

"Did you tell Ally what you overheard?"

"I had to. She caught me in the hall and wanted to know what was wrong."

He closed his eyes. With those words he'd

gone from joy to a new depth of despair in a matter of seconds.

"Are you angry at me?"

"No, sweetheart. But just so you know, I fell in love with Ally the moment I met her. In fact I loved her so much that when I heard she was only going to stay in Italy for one more day, I had to do something to keep her here."

"You mean like asking her to be my violin teacher?"

Gino smiled at her. "Exactly. In my fear of losing her at the end of the month, I'm afraid I rushed her into marriage before she was ready. As you know, she lost her husband a while ago and it would be understandable if she still had feelings for him. But I didn't want to wait for her to be my wife.

"I know I should have given her more time, but when you love someone as much as I love her, you're not thinking clearly.

"That's what I was telling Carlo when you happened to overhear us talking. He didn't know how I felt about Ally. All he knew was that I'd asked her to marry me because he thought I wanted you to have a mother.

"Sofia—do you know where she is?"

His niece studied him with those intelligent brown eyes of hers. "No, but you've got to find her, Uncle Gino!"

"Don't worry. I won't come back without her."

He flew out the door and down the hall to the stairs.

He almost had a heart attack when he discovered Ally coming up the stairs from the foyer.

She was composed as he'd ever seen her. Too composed.

"I was hoping you'd be here when I got back from Remo," she spoke before he could. "Tell me what I need to hear."

He knew what she was asking, but he wanted her to mean something else entirely different.

"All charges have been dropped against me. We're free, Ally."

"Thank heaven," she cried with her heart in her throat.

"It's all because of you. Now we can leave on our trip to Ischia."

"Sofia will be overjoyed."

He took another step towards her. "What about you?"

"You know I've been looking forward to it, but before we do anything, I need to talk to you."

His heart skipped several beats. "Then let's go to your room. It's closest."

He sensed her hesitation before she nodded.

Ally entered the room first and waited for him to shut the door.

"I hoped, but didn't dare to dream you'd be freed from suspicion this fast." He could tell she was breathing hard. "With this news, we can now discuss something that has been on my mind for a while."

Adrenaline riddled his body. "If it's about our marriage, you're my wife now and that's the way things are going to stay."

She eyed him with a calm that unnerved him.

"I want to stay married to you, too, Gino, but I just wanted you to know that you're free to live the way you did before we were married."

"I'm not sure I understand. I'm afraid you're going to have to spell that out for me."

She heaved a sigh. "If there's a woman you want to be with from time to time, I'll understand."

"You're talking about an open marriage?"

She averted her eyes. "Yes."

"Does that go for you, too?"

She paled. "Of course not. I plan to stay true to my wedding vows."

"But it's all right if I break mine, is that it?"

"As long as you're discreet, the eyes of the world will continue to view us as a married couple."

"So we are…"

She lifted a tremulous gaze to him once more. "I want your happiness, Gino."

"We went over all this before we got married. We agreed to stay married no matter what."

"But a lifetime is too long for a man like you who

can finally stop worrying about everyone else's needs and concentrate on your own for a change.

"I have no doubts there's a remarkable, marvelous woman out there somewhere waiting to meet a man like you. If and when that time comes, you can tell her the truth about us. If you decide to act on that love, you can do it knowing we had this conversation. You're an honorable man, Gino, but you'll be carrying it too far if you have to deny yourself a full life. I can't let our marriage stand in the way of your true happiness."

His hands formed fists. "Did you make this decision before you left the palazzo? Or after Sofia admitted eavesdropping on my conversation with Carlo?"

She didn't break eye contact with him. "Before."

She was lying, just the way she'd lied to him at the jail when she'd made that ridiculous confession in order to be set free. The fact was, she didn't have a dishonest bone in her body.

"What if I told you I want you in my bed."

"That doesn't surprise me."

Her answer stunned him.

"A man can sleep with his wife and the woman he really loves without much problem."

"Your husband did a lot of damage, but don't judge every man by his behavior."

"I'm not talking about Jim."

"I think you are," he challenged her. "That's what

I've been afraid of since I made up my mind I was going to marry you whether you were ready or not."

"Ready?"

He shifted his weight. "I know the kind of woman you are, Ally. You would never have married Jim if you hadn't been in love with him.

"You think I don't know that what he did has scarred you? But I was willing to take the chance that I could get you to love me like that one day.

"The only trouble is, in forcing marriage, I may have acted too soon. That's what I was telling Carlo, that I should have given you more time to get used to me.

"Unfortunately Sofia only heard the first part. If she'd stayed to hear the rest, she would know I fell hopelessly in love with you the night we met. I couldn't imagine life without you, so despite the risks, I got you to marry me first, and planned to spend the rest of my life finding ways to make you fall in love with me.

"When I repeated my vows before God, I meant every word of them, Ally. I love you more than my own life. If I can't get you to love me back, then I'd still rather live with you than anyone else. Do you understand what I'm saying?"

Her lovely body quivered in response. It defeated him more than any words she might have spoken.

"I've been a fool to hope for a miracle," his

voice grated. He started for the door, needing to get out of there.

"Don't leave, darling," she called to him. But she said it in Italian, not English.

In the next minute he was treated to words in his native tongue he never expected to hear pour from her lips and heart. When he turned in her direction, she came running toward him.

"I love you, Gino Di Montefalco." She threw her arms around his neck. "I love you more than I thought it was possible to love a man."

She covered his face and hair with kisses. "When I met Jim, I fell in love, but it didn't take long to realize he didn't have the substance I'd endowed him with. Somewhere along the way my love died. Maybe he sensed it before he ever met Donata. I'll never know the answer to that, but I do know that the night I met you changed my entire life."

She cupped his face in her hands, staring up at him with adoring green eyes.

"Do you honestly think I would have agreed to marry you if I hadn't wanted it with all my heart and soul?

"Oh, Gino— Love me, darling. It seems like a century that I've been waiting for you."

Ally waited impatiently for her husband to wake up.

The sun had risen above the horizon. The birds

were singing. The marvelous scent of lavender filtered through the open window of her room.

She lay facing him with their legs entwined.

They'd never made it up the stairs to his suite. In their desperate desire to love each other, they'd never come out of her room.

She knew he needed sleep. After being up all night while he'd been in Rome, only to spend all of last night making love to her, he deserved his rest.

But she was so on fire for him, it was impossible not to touch him.

He had silky black lashes she loved to feel against her cheek. Even in sleep his mouth had a sensuous curve that turned her blood molten.

He held her possessively. If she tried to move, she would waken him. Part of her was tempted. Maybe just one little kiss wouldn't hurt.

The second she pressed her mouth to his, he responded with breathtaking urgency. Then his eyes opened and she saw the flame of desire burning in their black depths.

"Buon giorno, bellissima," he said deep in his throat.

"Buon giorno, Apollo mio."

"Apollo?" he questioned, pulling her on top of him.

When she explained what she meant, he laughed triumphantly. When he did that, she thought she'd die with love for him.

He sobered for a moment. "I wish I'd met you when you were eighteen."

"Why eighteen?" she teased, tracing the line of his male mouth with her fingertip.

"You would have been old enough for me to carry you off without fear of the law coming after me."

She buried her face in his neck. "I know how you feel. So many years have already gone by. How is it you never married? You've never really told me."

He wrapped her closer in his arms. "I was waiting for you."

"Be serious, my love."

"I'm deadly serious," he came back with that hint of steel in his voice.

"In my teens and early twenties, I enjoyed women as much as the next man and didn't feel the need to settle down yet.

"After Marcello married Donata and I saw the way it was going, I thanked providence I was still a free man. That is until I met you.

"Your physical beauty attracted me immediately. Couple that with your defiance and your loyalty to my brother, a man you'd never even met, and I knew I'd met my soul mate. The trick was to get you to feel the same way about me."

She kissed him with passion, no longer afraid to express her love.

When he finally let her up for air she said, "No

trick was needed. The moment I emerged from the door of the *pensione* and saw you standing there like some proud, fierce Italian prince, I felt my whole soul quake."

He chuckled before giving her a long, hard kiss she felt to her toenails. "I like the way you talk, Signora Di Montefalco. The sun god and an Italian prince. What about just plain old Gino the farmer?"

She searched his eyes. "You're so many things, there aren't enough adjectives in the world to describe you."

So saying, she switched to Italian and told him she loved him.

She heard his sharp intake of breath. "Who taught you so well, you don't sound like a foreigner."

She kissed his eyelids. "My new daughter."

"Sofia's a little monkey. She held that bit of information back from me."

"I asked her to keep it a secret."

Gino suddenly moved so she was lying on her back. He stared down at her with fire in his eyes.

"Speaking of our niece, I think it's time we concentrated on producing a male heir just to keep the balance."

Ally smiled up at him. "If it's a girl we'll call her Gina and just keep trying until we get our own little Marcello."

Gino's eyes went suspiciously bright before his mouth fell on hers. She responded with the hunger of a woman who loved her husband beyond all else.

EPILOGUE

"CAN we swim a little longer, Mama?"

Ally checked her watch. "Ten more minutes. Then I need to get back to the house to feed the baby."

Two months had gone by since their precious Marcello had entered the world. Now Ally was determined to get her figure back. At this point she was within five pounds of her goal, but it was hard with Bianca's cooking always tempting her to eat more.

Gino had offered to come home at lunch to tend the baby. Father and son needed some playtime together.

If ever a man was made for fatherhood, it was her husband.

Little Marcello, who looked like his namesake, had already twisted his father around his baby finger.

The farmhouse was such a happy place, Ally felt like she was living in paradise.

When Gino had put it to a vote, no one wanted to live at the palazzo.

It would remain in the family until Sofia decided what to do with it.

The weather was already warm for the first of June. It was hard to believe that a year ago this month she'd come to Montefalco where Gino and a new thrilling life awaited her.

With Tomaso Castiglione behind bars for his crime, the horrific trauma of the past was over. Best of all, Sofia had been spared the details.

Feeling alive and glowing, Ally got out of the river and threw on a lightweight robe over her bikini.

Sofia's naturally curly hair was cut short these days. It only needed a brisk toweling to look perfect.

In the last year she'd grown into a young teen who was starting to resemble Donata more and more.

Sofia kept pictures of her mother in her room. Donata had been a beauty all right, and her daughter was following in her footsteps.

The two of them got in the truck and headed for home. With Sofia being such an excellent tutor, they talked mainly in Italian.

It made a huge difference when Ally helped out at the flower stand. Of course it would take years to talk and sound like Gino, but that was her goal.

She loved the language and the country. She loved his family. She adored *him*.

Hoping he would be able to stay while she nursed the baby, she drove faster than usual.

"Look, Mama—there's a taxi driving away from the house."

"You're right!"

Ally couldn't imagine who'd dropped by. She slowed to a stop and parked the truck around the side, hoping their visitor wouldn't be able to see her looking like this.

They hurried into the kitchen, then stopped. Ally's mother sat at the table next to Gino, feeding the baby his bottle. Her husband trapped Ally's gaze with a silent message before she cried, "Mom—"

Her mother's dark blond head lifted. She wore a smile that transformed her.

"Oh, honey— I shouldn't have waited so long to come. My little grandson's adorable."

Though Ally had invited her mother to come many times, she'd never taken her up on it. But with a new baby in the house...

Ally's eyes filled. "He and Sofia are the light of our lives. Mom? I'd like you to meet my daughter, Sofia."

"Come around here, honey," her mother said to Gino's niece. "I need to get to know both my grandchildren."

"Just a minute, Grandma. I've got to get something for you."

"For me?"

"Yes. I made it last summer and have been saving it for you. I'll be right back."

Ally had an idea where she was going. Taking advantage of the time, she hurried around the table and hugged her mom and the baby.

Her mother studied her. "You look wonderful, honey. Obviously marriage to this man agrees with you."

With those words her mother had let her know she'd put the past behind her and was ready to move on.

"He's the most wonderful thing that ever happened to me." Her voice shook with emotion.

Gino pulled her onto his lap.

"Careful, darling, I'm wet after just getting out of the river."

"I like you exactly like this," he whispered, kissing the side of her neck.

Sofia came back in the kitchen and walked around to Ally's mother. She carried a sheaf of dried flowers wrapped in cellophane and tied with ribbon.

"Lavender—" she cried. "Just the way my mother used to preserve it for gifts."

Tears welled in her gray eyes.

Ally took the baby so her mother could hug Sofia. "Thank you, honey. This is a priceless gift."

"Mama taught me how to do it. I have my own little sticker on it. See?"

Ally's mother looked closer. "Sofia's Scents. That's brilliant." She kissed her cheeks.

"Oh, Ally—" She turned to her. "I begged Edna to fly over with me, but she said I should come alone the first time."

"There'll be other times, Mom."

Gino hugged her tighter around the waist, baby and all. At least he could reach around her now. The thought gave Ally no end of satisfaction.

"We're hoping you'll move here permanently," Gino said to her mother. "You and your sister can have the run of the palazzo if you'd like."

"I'd love it if you and Aunt Edna lived here, Mom. I've missed you so much. You're the children's only grandparents. You'd be so proud of Sofia."

She turned to Sofia. "Darling? Go get your instrument and play something for Grandma."

"Okay." She ran out of the kitchen.

"My wife's been teaching her the violin. I understand I have you to thank for Ally blessing this house with music."

Her mother was genuinely overcome. "What a beautiful thing to say."

Soon Sofia returned and played several pieces that showed she was no beginner.

When she'd finished, Ally's mother got out of the chair to hug her. "If you keep this up, you're going to be able to play like Ally."

"I hope so."

"Is there a piano in the house?"

Sofia nodded. "In the living room."

"Then let's take a look at your music and I'll accompany you."

Ally got to her feet. "While you do that, I'll put the baby back to bed and get changed."

Gino kept his arm around her shoulders as they climbed the stairs.

By the time she'd put the baby in his crib, the strains of Mendelssohn reached the third floor.

Gino had the shower ready and waiting for her.

She stepped under the spray, waiting for him to shut the door, but he kept it open and simply watched her.

No matter how intimate they'd been, she still blushed.

"You're more gorgeous than ever. I never want to go to work."

"I never want you to go."

"I'm glad your mother finally came."

"So am I."

"This house feels normal, the way my parents' once did."

"Mine never felt quite normal because Mom was so unhappy." She reached for the towel he kept just out of reach.

"Gino—" she begged.

He finally relented and wrapped it around her.

"I didn't see any shadows in her eyes just now."

"Neither did I."

"The two of them are going strong downstairs, and our son is asleep."

"The answer is yes," Ally cried, so out of breath with longing, it was embarrassing.

He picked her up in his arms and carried her to the bed.

"This is what heaven is all about," he whispered against her lips moments later. "When Marcello was diagnosed, I didn't think I'd ever be happy again."

His fingers tightened in her damp curls. "You came into my life when I least expected it."

"You'll never know how happy I was when you showed up on the train and whisked me away to the farmhouse."

"Carlo had ordered me to make you go back to the States, but I couldn't allow you to do that." He devoured her mouth once more. "I couldn't stay away from you, *bellissima*."

"I hoped that was the reason," she whispered shakily.

"Now no more talk or your mother will think we're inconsiderate hosts."

"She knows what we're doing, Gino darling. I'm pretty sure she wants to make up for lost time, so let's give her her wish. Maybe I can grant you your wish at the same time."

"I have everything I want," he asserted.

She smiled at him. "Not everything. I was thinking we could work on another bambino to keep Marcello company and help you on the farm."

His eyes gleamed. "I believe in that kind of work. I'll give you fair warning. I'm prepared to work day and night, plus overtime."

"I think I'll put that in writing," she teased.

"You won't have to, Ally. I'll always come running home to you. Don't you know that yet?"

Oh, yes. She knew. And for the rest of their lives, she'd be waiting...

Join Mills & Boon® Tender Romance™ as the doors to the Bella Lucia restaurant empire are opened!

We bring you...

The Brides of Bella Lucia

A family torn apart by secrets, reunited by marriage

**There's double the excitement in August 2006!
Meet twins Rebecca and Rachel Valentine**

Having the Frenchman's Baby – Rebecca Winters
Coming Home to the Cowboy – Patricia Thayer

**Then join Emma Valentine as she gets a
royal welcome in September**
The Rebel Prince – Raye Morgan

Take a trip to the Outback and meet Jodie this October
Wanted: Outback Wife – Ally Blake

**On cold November nights catch up with
newcomer Daniel Valentine**
Married under the Mistletoe – Linda Goodnight

Snuggle up with sexy Jack Valentine over Christmas
Crazy About the Boss – Teresa Southwick

**In the New Year join Melissa as she heads off
to a desert kingdom**
The Nanny and the Sheikh – Barbara McMahon

**And don't miss the thrilling end to the Valentine
saga in February 2007**
The Valentine Bride – Liz Fielding

MILLS & BOON

www.millsandboon.co.uk

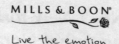

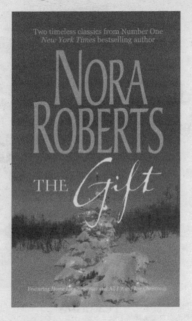

FREE!

4 Books
and a surprise gift!

We would like to take this opportunity to thank you for reading this Mills & Boon® book by offering you the chance to take FOUR more specially selected titles from the Romance series absolutely FREE! We're also making this offer to introduce you to the benefits of the Mills & Boon® Reader Service™—

★ **FREE home delivery**
★ **FREE gifts and competitions**
★ **FREE monthly Newsletter**
★ **Exclusive Reader Service offers**
★ **Books available before they're in the shops**

Accepting these FREE books and gift places you under no obligation to buy, you may cancel at any time, even after receiving your free shipment. Simply complete your details below and return the entire page to the address below. You don't even need a stamp!

YES! Please send me 4 free Romance books and a surprise gift. I understand that unless you hear from me, I will receive 6 superb new titles every month for just £2.80 each, postage and packing free. I am under no obligation to purchase any books and may cancel my subscription at any time. The free books and gift will be mine to keep in any case.

N6ZEF

Ms/Mrs/Miss/Mr ....Initials ....
BLOCK CAPITALS PLEASE
Surname ....
Address ....
....
....Postcode ....

Send this whole page to:
UK: FREEPOST CN81, Croydon, CR9 3WZ